PRAISE F...
The Story of G...

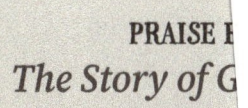

'A captivating, beautiful story that I feel sure will
bring joy into the hearts of many, many readers'
SOPHIE ANDERSON, author of
The House with Chicken Legs

—

'A gem of an adventure that stayed with me days
after finishing . . . beautifully written and imagined –
a future classic filled with heart and hope'
TIM TILLEY, author of Harklights

—

'Big hearted and beautiful, lyrical and lovely
with writing that flows like the river itself'
ZILLAH BETHELL, author of The Shark Caller

—

'I loved this timeless, moving story of
a deep connection with nature'
SARAH LEAN, author of The Good Bear

—

'Gorgeously magical, epic, and emotionally
powerful. I loved it so much!'
STEPHANIE BURGIS, author of
The Dragon with a Chocolate Heart

Also by Holly Webb

Magical Venice Series

The Maskmaker's Daughter
The Water Horse
The Mermaid's Sister
The Girl of Glass

Rose Series

Rose
Rose and the Lost Princess
Rose and the Magician's Mask
Rose and the Silver Ghost

Lily Series

Lily
Lily and the Shining Dragons
Lily and the Prisoner of Magic
Lily and the Traitor's Spell

The Story of Greenriver Series

The Story of Greenriver
The Swan's Warning

THE SWAN'S WARNING

A GREENRIVER STORY

HOLLY WEBB

Illustrated by ZANNA GOLDHAWK

Orion

ORION CHILDREN'S BOOKS

First published in Great Britain in 2023 by Hodder & Stoughton

1 3 5 7 9 10 8 6 4 2

Text copyright © Holly Skeet, 2023
Illustration copyright © Zanna Goldhawk, 2023

The moral rights of the author and illustrator have been asserted.

All characters and events in this publication, other than those clearly
in the public domain, are fictitious and any resemblance to
real persons, living or dead, is purely coincidental.

In order to create a sense of setting, some names of real places have been
included in the book. However, the events depicted in this book are imaginary
and the real places used fictitiously.

All rights reserved.

No part of this publication may be reproduced, stored in
a retrieval system, or transmitted, in any form or by any means, without
the prior permission in writing of the publisher, nor be otherwise circulated
in any form of binding or cover other than that in which it is published
and without a similar condition including this condition being
imposed on the subsequent purchaser.

A CIP catalogue record for this book
is available from the British Library.

ISBN 9781 51010 972 8

Typeset in ITC Century by Palimpsest Book Production Limited, Falkirk, Stirlingshire

Printed and bound in Great Britain by Clays Ltd, Elcograf S.p.A.

The paper and board used in this book are made
from wood from responsible sources.

Orion Children's Books
An imprint of
Hachette Children's Group
Part of Hodder & Stoughton Limited
Carmelite House
50 Victoria Embankment
London EC4Y 0DZ

An Hachette UK Company

www.hachette.co.uk
www.hachettechildrens.co.uk

For Jon, Ash, Robin and Will

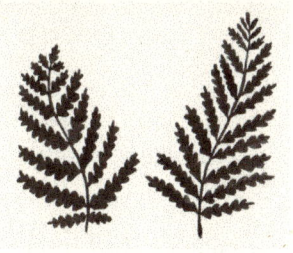

CHAPTER ONE

The two young otters chased each other in and out of the shallows, casting up fans of glittering water droplets. Sedge galloped after his sister, snatching at her tail with dark claws, until she wheeled round and leaped for the pale soft fur at his throat.

'Mmmf! Get off! I surrender,' he squeaked, trying to scrabble out of her grip by rolling into the water.

Silken pinned him for a moment longer and then sprang away, shooting out into the deeper channel of the river. She waited there, smirking at him, and Sedge paddled after her resentfully. 'Wait until I'm bigger than you,' he muttered. 'I will be, soon.'

'Then I'll just be faster.' Silken swirled around and under him, poking at his belly with sneaky paws, then popping back out of the water before he had time to grab her. 'See?'

Sedge growled, but he only half meant it. Silken hadn't grown up at Greenriver Holt, and she'd missed out on the otter cubs' chase games and wrestling matches – he couldn't blame her for enjoying herself now. If she'd tried to wrestle with the beaver kits at the Stronghold, they would have squashed her, or so Sedge gathered. Beavers were bigger and heavier than otters, although still very good swimmers.

Silken and Sedge had been separated as cubs, when the river had flooded the otter holt and swept them out of their sleeping chamber and into the roaring waters. Sedge had been rescued by his family, but Silken had washed up far down the river, close to the beaver lodge, and they had adopted her. Silken's desperate fight for survival had washed away all her otter memories, and she had grown up thinking of herself as a strange, small beaver, the disappointing daughter of the lodge's most respected builder. As the other young beavers grew stronger, Silken had faded into the background, knowing that she didn't fit in. She had tried to hide her singing voice and the songs that bubbled out of her. Beavers did not sing.

But it was a song that had brought the two cubs back together – the name song that Silken had made for them when they were still tiny, and she was still Elderberry, the adored daughter of the lady of the holt. The heir. That song had stayed with Silken all the time she was exiled as a little stranger at the lodge.

Ripe black elderberries,
Gleaming in the sun.
Ripe black elderberries,
Enough for everyone.

Pale dry sedge grass,
In the wind it sings,
Pale dry sedge grass,
Whispers secret things.

One spring morning, Silken had sung it to an inquisitive bird far down the river, and the song had travelled back upstream, chirruped from branch to nest to swaying reedy perch until two of Sedge's young companions at the holt, Lily and Tormentil, had heard it from a willow warbler.

Lily and Tormentil had sung the catchy song to each other while they were all resting on the riverbank, and Sedge had heard his sister's words for the first time since she'd disappeared. It was *their* song, their very own – and it was then that Sedge had known Elderberry must still be alive.

Now his sister nuzzled at him gently and her stubby whiskers flickered against his fur. Sedge rolled over in the water, floating belly up in the bright spring sun. Silken sighed and slowly sculled her paws beside him.

'What is it?' Sedge murmured. The sun was warming the surface of the water so that it slipped over his coat like honey. He peered at Silken through half-closed eyes. 'What's the matter?'

Silken stopped paddling, hunching up one shoulder. She looked away from him.

'What? You were so happy a moment ago.' Sedge huffed. 'Oh. Maybe you weren't.' She had been distracting herself with their wild game. He rolled upright and then turned nose over paws into the deep cool of the river to wake up. 'Tell me,' he spluttered, surfacing again next to his sister. Then he swallowed and added quietly, 'Do you want to go back to the lodge?'

Silken gave her half-shrug again.

'You did say you were only coming upstream to see what the holt was like,' Sedge muttered. 'I suppose now you have.'

'I don't *want* to go back.' She coiled round, snapping her teeth on the fine hairs at the end of her tail. 'But I'm not sure that I want to be here either. Maybe I don't want to be anywhere,' she added angrily. 'I'm just a misfit.'

Sedge smirked. 'You said it, not me.'

'Hey!'

Sedge tugged his sister to the bank, where they scrambled out on to the thin turf. 'I thought you were happy,' he said, shaking himself dry. 'I know it's hard work doing the repairs after the flood, but you didn't seem to mind . . .'

Silken rolled, squeezing the water out of her fur. 'I don't. It's nothing like the work we used to have to do to keep the lodge secure. No one's asking me to fell trees and swim them down the river, are they? Besides, I'd be doing the same work back there – my father's letter said the flood damaged the Stronghold too. It isn't the work. It's – it's the way everyone looks at me.'

'You did come back from the dead,' Sedge pointed out. 'And then you sang to Lady River and she listened. The whole holt saw it! You sang to her and she drew back the floodwaters.' He nudged her gently. 'Mind you, I'd have liked it more if you'd asked Lady River to clear the mud away as well, but I'll settle for a holt without any water in it—'

'Everyone stares at me,' Silken whispered. 'And they remember things that I don't. When Bramble the cook gave us the gathering bags for the crayfish traps this morning, he told me that he knew how much I love elderberry syrup. He said he'd be able to rescue some from the store chambers.' She looked worriedly at Sedge. 'I don't know what elderberry syrup tastes like!'

'It'll come back to you,' Sedge said soothingly. 'And if you don't like it, I'll have it. Bramble never gives me treats, just jobs to do. I'd make the most of it while you can; he'll have you shelling great piles of crayfish soon enough.'

'You're meant to shell them?' Silken said anxiously. She glanced down at the woven-rush gathering bag strapped around her middle, bulging with her haul of crayfish. 'I've just been crunching them up and spitting the hard bits out. Is that wrong?'

'It isn't wrong,' Sedge told her. 'Bramble likes to fussy food up. I munch crayfish straight from the water if I want a little something midday, of course I do. But if he's making a great dishful for dinner, for everyone, he wants them shelled. Especially when it's a great feast like tonight. Don't worry yourself.'

Silken sighed. 'I don't know these things. Beavers don't eat fish, or crayfish, or even beetles. I don't know how an otter ought to be.'

Sedge laid one paw over hers. 'Only because you haven't been taught it. I had to be taught *everything*. All the time. At least when we're busy clearing up flood damage no one can chase us for lessons. I must be due days of history and weather patterns and herb lore. Let alone manners and ritual. I'm keeping out of Teasel's way.' He nudged his sister. 'Once everything's back to rights, she'll growl at you too.'

Silken nodded. Teasel was their mother's chief counsellor

and dearest companion, and she had been a second parent to Sedge all his life. She had also been the first of the Greenriver otters to meet them on their return to the holt, and in a fury of love and worry she had taken Sedge by the scruff of his neck and shaken him. Silken had snarled at the old otter, telling Teasel to let her brother go – the first time she had claimed Sedge as family.

At the beaver lodge she would never have dared to speak to an elder so sharply, but she had been exhausted and frightened. After that, lessons with Teasel had seemed a daunting prospect.

'Should we go back?' she asked, nodding upriver towards the holt. 'Bramble said he wanted the crayfish in good time.'

'Mmm,' Sedge agreed. 'And there'll be more sweeping mud out of storerooms. Still, I noticed some of the labels have rubbed off the jars on the lower shelves. It would be a good deed if we tested them for Bramble, wouldn't it?'

'Happy to help, that's you,' Silken said with a grin, as they slipped back into the sun-warmed water.

As Sedge and Silken rounded the curve of the river, they saw that the holt under the willow tree was surrounded by a flurry of busy otter figures. It made Sedge's stomach twist inside him, remembering that same view four days before, when he and Silken had fought their way back up the flooded waterway and found the holt marooned, with not a single otter to be seen. Things still felt so fragile – but Lady River had promised them, hadn't she? No more floods . . .

'Silken! Silken!' Two tiny furry bodies flung themselves into the water from a willow tree root, paddling splashily towards them.

Sedge chuckled, nudging his sister. 'Told you. You're their favourite person now.'

Silken pulled up in the water, eyeing Willow and Marigold nervously. She still wasn't used to the little otters and their extravagant love. At the beaver lodge, kits had been kept close by their mothers – which had made motherless Silken an even stranger child.

'Will you come and play with us?' Marigold begged, pawing hopefully against Silken's side.

'Sing us more songs?' Willow added.

'We've got to take these to Bramble.' Silken looked round at Sedge for help, but her brother only wrinkled his muzzle, laughing at her.

'Bramble won't mind waiting a bit longer.'

'You can play too,' Willow said, launching herself at Sedge and squirming up on to his back. 'Oooh! You've got bigger while you were away. Swim, Sedge!'

Marigold immediately clawed her way on to Silken's

shoulders, and the two little otters bounced and squeaked in delight as Sedge and Silken swam them back towards the holt.

'Faster! Go faster!'

'Ooof, can't . . . I'm sinking . . .' Sedge panted, sinking lower in the water as they came close to the knotted roots of the great tree. 'Willow, you're too big . . .' He blew a string of bubbles and then did a slow and graceful roll. Willow slid off his back and landed on a tree root looking indignant.

'Awww, Sedge. I wanted more rides!'

Marigold leaped down from Silken's shoulders into the water and Willow followed her. The small cubs exchanged a sneaky glance, then set up a flurry of splashing at Silken and Sedge, sending clouds of spray flying all around them.

Silken spluttered, twisting away, but Sedge retaliated, sending a wave over the little ones. 'Silken, help me get them!'

His sister hesitated. Should she? The cubs seemed so little – but she supposed, if Sedge was doing it . . .

She swung her tail, flicking spray up the cubs' noses. They squealed delightedly and thrashed the water with their small paws. Silken shook herself wildly and splashed and scooped and kicked, yelping and squeaking as loudly as the others.

Until she twisted round and saw her mother perched on the tree root, looking lovingly down at her. Silken just about managed not to send a pawful of water over Lady Thorn's silvery muzzle, but it was close. She gasped, and froze.

Silken watched her mother's eyes darken. She had seen Silken flinch away. She had seen that her daughter didn't dare splash water at her – that she didn't know her well enough to play with her.

'I'm sorry . . .' They both whispered it at once, and Sedge and the two little cubs drew back, aware of the tension between mother and daughter.

'We've a good catch of crayfish,' Sedge murmured at last, just to break the silence.

Their mother took a breath and nodded. 'Good. Bramble's already terrorising the kitchen, complaining that half his stores are flood-soaked, and he can't possibly be expected to create a feast worthy of the holt and Lady River. Crayfish might cheer him up.' She patted a paw affectionately against Sedge's muzzle, and then, rather uncertainly, did the same to Silken.

Sedge groaned. 'He'll probably make us shell the crayfish. Unless there's anything else you want doing?' he added hopefully.

Lady Thorn shook her head. 'No. Go along and help Bramble.'

Sedge bowed his head politely to their mother and led Silken and the two small cubs into the holt, making for the kitchen.

'About time,' muttered the sentry at the main entrance, a young she-otter with particularly sharp teeth. 'I can hear Bramble cursing from here. You should have been back with those crayfish ages ago.'

'We were busy emptying the traps,' Sedge protested. 'We've both got a huge bag.' But all four of them sped up, galloping through the main hall and out to the kitchen, which was hollowed into the back of the hill behind the willow tree.

'Finally!' Bramble roared as they piled in. 'Where have you *been*? I've had the herb broth simmering so long, it's practically boiled dry!' He waved a paw dramatically at Sedge and Silken's bags. 'Don't just stand there,' he told his assistants, 'get them cooking! We need everything ready for the feast before the ceremony starts.'

Several hot-and-bothered-looking otters seized the bags and tipped great heaps of dark, shining crayfish into a huge clay platter. They piled them up so high that the catch spilled between delicate dishes of pickled collops of pike and poached river trout so pink and fresh that Sedge longed to steal a pawful.

The crayfish were plunged into a cauldron of broth and then ladled out again scarlet and shining. A sweet scent of herbs and fish floated across the kitchen, and Silken's stomach growled.

'Get to work!' Bramble pushed a dish of boiled crayfish into Silken's paws, and then eyed Willow and Marigold sharply. At last he reached out to chuck each of them under the chin, and nodded. 'Here. You can sit under the table, and Sedge will show you how to shell crayfish. You're never too young to learn, and from what I understand, young Silken here needs teaching too.'

Sedge ducked under the table and the little cubs scrambled after him, peering out at the busy paws hurrying around the kitchen.

'Here . . .' Sedge picked up a crayfish and held it out. He and Silken had dispatched them with a neat bite between the head and the thorax, but other than that they were whole – and cased in armour, with vicious-looking claws. Now he bit the head off entirely and spat it at Marigold, making her squeak.

'Don't be mean,' Willow said severely. 'And that's just messy.' She put the head into a bowl of scraps. 'Now what?'

'Pull the tail back, and then off, you see?' Sedge ran a claw up the side of the brownish body and hooked out the pale meat. 'Done. Only a couple of hundred more to go.' He pushed the pile of crayfish towards Silken and the youngsters and they set to work, carefully biting and ripping away the shells.

Bramble peered under the table and tipped another load of scarlet crayfish into their dish. 'Hurry up! Small paws shell quickest, and remember I've eyes in the end of my tail. No sneaky gobbling!'

Marigold's eyes bulged. 'How did he know?' she whispered. 'I only wanted a taste.'

Sedge snorted. 'He always does. But he's only playing at being grumpy. There'll be a treat in it for you when you've finished.'

The little cub brightened up, but she did keep looking over her shoulder at Bramble's tail, broad with muscle. The very tip of it was curled under the table, as if the cook really was watching them. At last the four cubs crawled out and Marigold held up a dish of neatly peeled crayfish tails. It was about a third of the size of the pile of shells and bits and whiskers in the bowl.

'Ah, very nice, very nice . . .' Bramble murmured, picking them over with a hooked black claw. 'I shall tell Lady Thorn who shelled the crayfish for her soup at the feast. Hurry along now, out of my way.' His gaze landed on Silken. 'Ah! Just a moment.' He scurried into the nearest storeroom and returned with a large clay jar. 'The only jar of this I could find that hadn't spoiled. Elderberry syrup. Do you remember it?' He eyed her hopefully, his head on one side.

Silken nodded slowly. 'I wasn't sure, but now I think so! I remember that huge jar . . . But I was so small . . .'

'Of course you were, smaller than these two.'

'I *love* elderberry syrup!' Marigold breathed, gazing hopefully at the jar.

Elderberries were plentiful along the riverbank, but it took a great many berries and a lot of honey to make very little syrup, so it was a rare treat. All the young otters watched greedily as Bramble dipped in a little wooden ladle and poured a dash of dark, sticky syrup into four tiny wooden cups. He handed them each a cup and stood back, watching as Silken breathed in the heady summer-autumn scent and then delicately poked the tip of her tongue into the dark sweetness.

It was as if time washed away. Silken thought she had been left with no memories of the holt at all – whether because of the terror of last spring's flood, or the cold water, or a head injury, she didn't know. She had accepted that she was never going to understand exactly what had happened. She knew the facts, of course – that she and Sedge had been swept out of their soft reed bed and dragged into the dark floodwaters. Lady Thorn and the other otters had searched for them desperately, and at last Teasel had caught Sedge up out of the flood and saved him. But Silken – or Elderberry, as she was known then – had been hurled further down the river, washing up in a great swan's nest, many days' journey away. She had been a tiny, bedraggled cub, and the swan hadn't known what to do with her. He had taken her to the nearest furred creatures he knew, the beavers. The Stronghold.

Silken had been renamed and had grown up among the beavers, small and strange and misunderstood, even though her adoptive father had loved her dearly. All the things that made her an otter – the acrobatic swimming, her hunting instincts, her eerie singing voice – they were the things that the beavers couldn't understand, and the things that Silken couldn't seem to give up. It was only a chance encounter with the raft otters, a travelling merchant band, that had let Silken see that she wasn't some strange sort of runt. Her family had been lying to her, and they weren't her family at all.

She had set off up the river the very next day, to find where she had come from.

Now the taste of elderberries and love swept Silken into a flood of returning memories. For a moment she was sure she could feel her mother's fur against her own. She knew suddenly that the last time she'd had elderberry syrup she and Sedge had been curled together on the riverbank in a patch of sunlight, nuzzled against their mother's side. The sun had been warm on her coat, and the syrup so thick and sweet that it had coated her mouth. They had played in the water, splashing and squeaking . . .

'She does remember,' Bramble said quietly, and Silken

blinked at the others, surprised to find herself in the hot, dim kitchen again. She had been messing about in the shallows, in the sunlight . . .

'Food and stories,' Bramble said, his eyes bright. 'They're always a way back.'

Silken nodded uncertainly. She was trying to hold on to the memory of Ma's warm, loving expression from that day long ago. Silken wanted to replace the sadness in Ma's eyes earlier in the afternoon with that old warmth.

Perhaps Bramble was right, and there was a way back for them both. They could be mother and daughter again. After all, she had called her mother Ma, she realised, even if it was only to herself.

CHAPTER TWO

When they had finished their syrup, Bramble collected the little wooden cups and nodded to Silken and the others. 'Off with you now, go and get yourselves ready for the ceremony. I don't need you all under my paws.' He shooed them away with a flick of his claws and the young otters raced out to the river again to rinse away the shells and grease and smell of crayfish.

Willow and Marigold's mothers happened to be out on the bank, helping to string long garlands of flowers through the willow branches.

'Silken!' Marigold's mother chuckled. 'I told you they'd find her,' she murmured to Willow's mother. She turned to Silken again. 'You and Sedge are all they talk about. Thank you for being so patient with them.'

Silken was sure the two mothers exchanged a thoughtful glance. Sedge had told her she'd end up saddled with the cubs all the time if she could sing them to sleep, and it looked like he was right. Silken resolved to be less friendly the next time she saw the small otters . . . but they were funny, and sweet, and she loved the way they snuggled into her fur. She wasn't sure she could bring herself to snub them. And they did make a very good audience when she was trying to come up with a song.

'Do we have to wear wreaths again for this ceremony?' she asked Sedge as they wriggled and scrubbed in the shallows. How had she managed to get crayfish whiskers in her ear?

'Ha. No.' Sedge grinned at her, showing his teeth. 'They wouldn't stay on. This is more like a celebration than a ritual – a thanksgiving, you could say, for the turning back of the waters and the sight of Lady River. We don't have it very often – the last time was when the raft otters visited, when we were celebrating our friendship.'

'Hey! You two!' Teasel called, waving them over. 'You're nippy enough, Sedge. Can you scramble up the tree?' She pointed to a willow basket full of tiny oil lamps. 'Your mother wants them set out all along the branches. Like glow-worms, she says.' Teasel sighed. 'Lot of nonsense.' But she spoke fondly. 'You think you two can get up there?'

Beavers did not climb trees. Silken had never tried such a thing. But the bark of the old willow was deeply ridged, and her claws were strong. She nodded.

Sedge looked at the tree with his head on one side, and said, 'You know what, Teasel, I slept in a tree, the first night I set off downriver.'

'Lady River help us,' Teasel muttered, as Sedge scrambled up the knotted trunk and Silken stretched after him, hooking her paws deep into the cracks.

'Did you really sleep in a tree?' Silken whispered as she scrabbled and heaved herself on to the first branch. They were already a good way above Teasel, and Sedge reached down to pull the willow basket up after them on its plaited rope.

'Yes. It had moss all up the branches; it was very comfortable,' Sedge told her primly. 'I knew it would annoy Teasel though – that's why I told her. She doesn't like us doing anything that otters haven't already done for ever, do you see?' He brushed a paw across his stubby whiskers. 'I used to worry about that a lot.'

Silken tucked a clay lamp into the crook of a branch and lit it with the tinder box, cupping her paw round the wick until a tiny flame flared up. She gazed at the flame, glowing softly in the low light of late afternoon. That way she didn't have to look at her brother. 'Leaving the Stronghold and travelling up the river changed everything for me,' she murmured. 'It's only since we've been back here that I've seen how much difference that journey made for you too.'

She felt Sedge sigh and shrug – the branch shuddered underneath them, and she dug her claws in hard.

'The holt changed while I was gone,' he said. 'I don't mean the flood damage. Everything's different.' He turned away from her, padding out along the branch to place another lamp, looking thoughtful. 'Or maybe the holt didn't change. I set off on my own, didn't I? There was no one telling me what to do, all that time. I had to make my own decisions. Find my own way. I suppose *I* was the one who changed.'

He was silent, and Silken wondered if he was remembering the flooded riverbank and the wolf who had pinned her into the mud – the wolf who had been haunting the banks of the river long before she and Sedge were born. They still hadn't told anyone at Greenriver that Sedge had killed her. Silken supposed that the news would travel up the riverbank eventually.

She wondered how much he thought about it. It came back to her often, in the middle of the night. The feeling of squirming in the mud. The darkness swirling up around her eyes, like silt stirred up into clear river water. And the dwindling warmth of the wolf's body stretched out beside her, life slowly seeping away into the mud. But Sedge must remember other things: the smooth weight of the rock between his paws, the sound it had made when he brought it down. That would change anyone.

She stretched out her paw for the tinder box to light the last little lamp. She let their paws meet, and he sighed again.

'I'll settle back into it,' he muttered. 'I have to. Or perhaps you'll take over and I won't have to,' he added, glancing sideways at her.

Silken snorted. 'I'm not going to become lady of the holt just so you can give up on all the duties you don't like and go off adventuring down the river.'

Sedge growled something rude and lowered the basket back to Teasel. Silken followed him carefully down the tree trunk, thinking to herself. She was older than Sedge, by a few minutes, so according to the traditions of the holt, she should be the otters' Lady, after her mother. The holt's leader.

Silken had understood that as a tiny cub. She'd accepted it as the way things were. Then she had been swept away downriver and grown up at the Stronghold. There, her adopted father had led the lodge, but only because he was a respected builder. He had been chosen, not born to rule.

When she and Sedge had first met on the riverbank and he had told her she was the heir, Silken had almost decided she was going nowhere near the holt. She'd spent long enough as a strange disappointment, and she didn't want it to happen all over again. Still, she'd let Sedge persuade her to come back with him, to meet her mother, to see what the holt was like. She'd told him she wasn't going take up her position as the heir again – but she hadn't told her mother that. Surely she didn't need to? How could they want an otter who'd grown up far down the river not even knowing that she *was* an otter leading their holt, just because she was the eldest? It was foolish. She wasn't acting on any of Sedge's hints.

She could speak to Lady Thorn. But she didn't even feel like her mother's daughter, not yet. They were still getting used to each other, getting to know one another again. How could she tell Lady Thorn that she might not want to stay, let alone lead the holt?

At the bottom of the tree they found Teasel peering up at the tiny lights, and their mother standing beside her looking delighted. 'You see, I told you,' she said. 'Like glow-worms. I've always loved glow-worms, but you can't persuade them to stay in one place for long enough.'

Silken brushed the bark dust out of her fur and gazed up at the tree. The lamps shone in the fading afternoon, bathing the tree in a soft golden light. It looked like something from a story, magical and strange.

Already the otters were gathering, pointing out the lamps and the flower garlands, chattering excitedly. Sedge's friend Lily – her friend too, Silken told herself fiercely – was swinging

Tormentil round in circles, and Willow and Marigold were hopping about. Teasel and Lady Thorn bowed deeply to each other and began to circle too, one paw held up high and the other tight behind their backs. Around them, the watching otters began to clap and stamp their paws.

'What are they *doing*?' Silken hissed to Sedge, forgetting that she was angry.

Sedge blinked at her. 'Dancing. Oh.' He shook his head. 'Beavers don't do that either?'

Silken drew in a breath to defend the lodge, to say that they were good at other things, but she was too entranced. All around the great willow tree, otters were nodding and bowing and parading in circles while others stamped and clapped. Bramble had emerged from the kitchen back door, trailing weary-looking helpers. He sighed delightedly, seeming to throw off the heat and stress of the kitchens, and seized Willow and Marigold's paws in his with a deep bow.

Willow squeaked delightedly and bowed back. They were so graceful, Silken thought, even with Bramble stooping to reach the small otters' paws.

'Is dancing another thing that otters are known for?' Silken whispered to her brother. 'Is it like singing?'

Sedge shook his head. 'No, no. We sing all the time, but dancing is mostly for feasts and celebrations. It's special.' He lifted his paws, frowning, as if he didn't know how to explain. 'And this is nothing yet. You'll see.'

Silken padded one paw on the damp ground. The stamping beat echoed inside her, and she longed to join the dance. But she didn't know the steps. The slow circles seemed easy enough, but she had a sense that they were only the beginning, like a fire about to catch. Then the dance would be wild and fast, and she would be left behind.

Does it matter? she thought fiercely. *They keep telling me I'm part of the holt. If they want me to stay, they'll have to let me learn things.*

Sedge was clapping along, hopping from paw to paw, and Silken couldn't help it. She twirled on the spot and Sedge let out a gleeful chuckle. He jumped over her whipping tail, seized her paw, and they began to dance with the others.

Sedge changed paws with a little half-bow and led her round the other way. He was humming, Silken realised, a low sound, sweet and stately.

'Please sing it,' she begged. 'Sing it with the words too.'

'There aren't any words now.' Sedge shook his head. 'Perhaps there were once, but now they're lost. There's only the music, and not much of that.' He picked up pace a little, and Silken tried to follow the others as they hopped and kicked.

'But . . . I know the words,' Silken said, her muzzle

wrinkling as she hustled around, always a step behind. The words were there in her head now, just waiting for her to sing them. She began, haltingly and in a half-whisper.

> *We dance on in a circle,*
> *Sweep past and then turn.*
> *Won't you join us, as we dance on*
> *Dance with us, in the sun.*
> *Give your paw to me,*
> *And lead me on then,*
> *Stepping onwards through the shadows,*
> *Dance with us, to the sun . . .*

Silken sped up, feeling the music carry her. The evening sunlight was warm on her fur as they stamped and twirled in and out of the dappled shadows. The great willow tree was coming into its full leaf now, and its branches seemed to swirl and sway with the dancing otters. The leaves whispered and hissed, and she could hear them in her song – a song that had been made for this place – for this tree, even. It belonged to them all. Silken shivered a little with happiness, remembering that it belonged to her too.

She kept singing, a little louder. Other otters were picking up the words now, murmuring them together, chittering delightedly as they fitted them to the tune and their dancing paws. Silken noticed the smiles and nods of approval and saw that Lady Thorn's eyes were shining.

The dancing otters circled faster and sang louder, until all at once they drew back to make one great half-circle. They danced to the very edge of the riverbank and then slipped gracefully into the water, one by one. Streams of bubbles floated up, and Silken realised that the dance had carried on under the surface. Sedge dived and she followed him, feeling the water slide over her fur and the bubbles rise. Deep in the main channel of the river, cold and slow, otters looped and turned. They swirled over and around one another in a pattern far more wild and free than anything they could make on land.

The music was still there, Silken thought, blinking to herself, as she swam after Sedge. She could feel it in the current and the waving of the weeds on the riverbed. The water sang to her, softly, sweetly: *Won't you join us, as we dance on, dance with us in the deep?*

The otters were twirling round one another now, passing on from partner to partner in a spiralling chain. Trying to follow the dance made Silken dizzy, but she loved it. She swung through the water patting paws and linking tails until she fetched up in front of a new otter, a taller, paler creature that

she didn't recognise. The silvery-white otter coiled around her so close that Silken felt the faint brush of her fur, smooth and chill.

Lady River.

How do you like your holt? Lady River murmured silently. *Do you know yet that you're an otter?*

I remember that I was an otter, once, Silken answered her cautiously. *I hope to be again.* She hesitated, and said more strongly, *I will be.*

You are, Lady River told her, and she faded away into the streams of bubbles.

Silken somersaulted, nose over tail, filled with a sudden glee. Sedge bobbed in front of her again, his eyes wide with questions, and jerked his head to beckon her out of the water. The otters were swimming back to the bank now, scrambling out and laughing.

Silken was almost the last out of the water. Some of the holt must have stayed behind on the riverbank or left the water dance early. Now there were tables set in the clearing all around the great willow tree, and Bramble's kitchen helpers were piling them high with dishes. The lights in the branches shone brightly now that the evening was drawing in, and Silken watched the otters from where she was standing between the river and the bank, part of the holt and not.

Sedge climbed out of the water behind her and started to groom his fur dry. He looked a little dazed. He must have seen Lady River too.

'Was that—' he started to say, then his voice died away – they both knew it had been, but it was hard to accept that the spirit of the river had come to dance with them. 'Ma's calling us.'

Lady Thorn was beckoning them to a table set close against the tree, indicating the seats either side of her, the places of honour. The whole holt was watching as they scurried to sit down.

Thorn waved a paw towards the dishes. 'Our thanks for this great feast,' she said, nodding to Bramble. 'A fitting celebration, now that the holt is almost back to how it should be. We thank Lady River for her gentle ways, and for her grace. She appeared among us. She spoke back the waters. We will not forget.'

'We will not forget . . .' soft whispers echoed back, and Thorn lifted her wooden cup, looking around at the gathered otters.

'A feast! We deserve this, after all our work. Be happy, and eat well.' She watched the otters passing dishes down the tables for a moment, then nudged Silken affectionately with her muzzle. 'My clever child,' she said, her voice low but full of pride. 'Those words! I've never heard them, but they sounded as though they'd always belonged to the dance.'

Silken nodded. None of the other otters had seen Lady River join the dance, she realised. That was an even greater miracle than a lost song found.

'I didn't make them up.' She frowned, trying to think how to explain. 'It was like I . . . *remembered* them. But I'm sure I'd never heard them before. It doesn't make much sense. They just . . . seemed to go with the dance.' She shifted uncomfortably, and stared down at the table. Her mother was gazing at her, and she knew that the other otters were watching her too. There was a hunger in their eyes, as though they wanted something from her. Silken wasn't sure she could give it to them.

'The cub has a great gift,' Teasel said over her head, and Silken glanced up worriedly. She kept imagining how Sedge must feel, with all this fuss being made over her. It didn't seem fair on him at all. She knew that he had been brought up as their mother's heir but that he'd always felt unworthy, as though he'd stolen Silken's place. Now his own tutor – who had always been so stern with him – was praising his sister. They were casting him aside, Silken thought, a tiny flame of anger starting to grow inside her.

Silken tried to catch his eye. She wanted to nudge him, to

make a face at him, to show him somehow that this wasn't what she wanted. But he was out of reach on her mother's other side and had his eyes fixed on the table. His ears were flat.

'We are truly fortunate,' Thorn murmured, gazing at Silken. 'Lady River gave us our hope again when she brought you back to us.'

Teasel nodded solemnly, and Sedge drooped even more. His whiskers were practically trailing on the table. Silken sat up straighter and glared. That was quite enough.

'It wasn't Lady River who brought me back,' she snapped, forgetting her shyness around her mother. 'It was Sedge. He was the one who came and found me! He went all the way down the river, *on his own*. No one else came to look for me,' she added pointedly. 'And he didn't dare tell you that he thought I was alive either.' She watched the worry creases around her mother's eyes and muzzle deepen, and felt guilty, but not guilty enough to keep quiet.

'A cub's foolish journey,' Teasel growled, and some of the older otters seated further along the table exchanged wise looks. Silken felt like growling at them. *How dare they?*

'He was right to go!' Thorn said, protesting, though not as hard as Silken thought she should have.

'Mmmm.' Teasel eyed Sedge sideways. 'He was. Though I suspect that wanting to head off downriver on an adventure played a part in his plan, journeying being more to his taste than lessons and chores.'

'I am here, you know,' Sedge muttered to his plate.

Teasel nodded. 'You are a dutiful son, Sedge. Nothing wrong with wanting to seek wilder waters, as long as you know your true place is at the holt. I told your mother that you'd be back by the full moon, in time for the ceremony – and so you were.'

Lady Thorn patted his paw. 'My dear, good cub. Teasel is quite right.'

'He isn't a dear, good cub!' Silken thumped her paw on the table. 'You make him sound as if he's still a nursling. He's a hero. He saved me!'

Sedge looked up sharply, realising what she was about to say. 'Silken, *ssshhh*! Don't!'

Silken fell silent. Thorn's eyes widened in surprise, but she seemed pleased. 'Your love for your brother is just as it should be,' she said gently. 'We do know how brave he was to make the journey to find you. I only meant that Lady River intended for him to bring you back to us. She took you, as a tiny cub, and then she brought you back. She guided Sedge on his journey.'

'Did she?' Silken demanded, leaning round to stare at Sedge. 'You didn't look very guided to me.'

'I don't know.' Sedge shrugged. 'Maybe. Most of the time I didn't really know what I was doing. Just that I was sure you must be along the river somewhere.'

'Of course she guided you,' said Teasel. 'As if you could have done such a thing alone.'

'He did do it alone!' shouted Silken, her temper rising again. The words were spilling out of her – but Sedge was wrong to keep this hidden! 'I wasn't talking about him finding me, anyway. I meant that he's a hero because he saved me from the wolf.'

A few of the closer otters had already been listening to their conversation. But now the hum of chatter among the tables died away, and even the whisper of the willow leaves seemed to hush. The clearing was full of silent, staring otters.

'The night wolf?' Lady Thorn hissed through her teeth. 'You *saw* her?'

Sedge stared down at the table again. Silken looked around at the shocked faces. 'He didn't just see her. He killed her.'

There was a moment more of silence, and then uproar. Otters surged from the benches, demanding to know what had happened. A few seemed to think that this was some sort of ridiculous joke. Silken shrank closer to her mother as a tall, dark-furred otter leaned over her, teeth bared. 'The night wolf isn't something for cubs to make stories of!' the dark otter snarled. 'I've seen the beast, loping along the bank. She left me fear-frozen. How dare you?'

'Crowfoot, step back,' Lady Thorn told him, her voice low. 'You're frightening her.'

Crowfoot shook his head. 'Spinning silly tales! If you'd seen her . . .' He fell back a little, shuddering.

'It isn't a story, I promise you.' Silken swallowed. 'Sedge killed her to protect me.'

Something in her thin, strained voice seemed to convince Crowfoot at last. He peered at her and nodded slowly. 'Tell us,' he growled. 'The whole story. Not one of your songs.'

Silken exchanged glances with Sedge, who sighed and nodded. She knew he hadn't wanted the story told, at least not yet. She felt guilty for letting it burst out of her. But she couldn't let them all dismiss him so easily.

'We were caught in the flood surge,' she began, as the otters leaned in to listen. 'Sedge was hit by a branch – I managed to dive out of the way at the last moment, but it caught him across the back of the head, and he was swept away.' She caught Lady Thorn's shiver, and laid her paw across her mother's. She saw Sedge do the same on the other side. 'He's here now, remember?' she whispered. 'We're both here.' She turned to look at Crowfoot again, forcing herself to meet his eyes.

'I found Sedge, but he'd been knocked out by the branch, and I wasn't sure he was breathing. I dragged him out of the current and laid him in the mud. I was trying to wake him up – I was desperate, hitting his muzzle, calling him. I needed him to come back to me.' She looked down at her paw lying on top of her mother's. 'I forgot to look out for any other danger. I didn't even hear her, until she was beside me. Until she spoke to me.' Silken let out a shuddering sigh, allowing herself to remember. She had pushed the whole experience deep down inside her, not wanting to see that shining golden eye peering into hers ever again.

'She pinned me down. She had her paw on my throat, squeezing the air out of me, and everything was misting over. I wanted to let go, just to make the heaviness on top of me go away. And then it did. The weight slipped off my chest and the wolf was lying there in the mud next to me. I watched her fade away to nothing, till she was just a ratty heap of fur.' Silken was silent for a moment. Then she looked round at Crowfoot, at her mother, at Teasel. Even Willow and Marigold were staring at her, their eyes wide with fear. 'Sedge had hit her with a rock. He killed her, for me.'

The watching otters turned to look at her brother now.

'Sedge . . .' Lady Thorn whispered. 'Is this true?'

Sedge nodded uncomfortably.

'Why would you not say?' Teasel demanded. 'This is news we should all have known.'

'We never kept it a secret,' Silken pointed out. 'How could we? There were birds telling it up and down the banks as soon as we left her there in the mud.'

Teasel's lip curled, showing clearly what she thought of that. 'You did not tell your holt.'

'I didn't want to.' Sedge glanced at their mother. 'It – it didn't feel like something to boast about. She was old, and sick . . .'

'She nearly killed both of us!' Silken snapped. 'You had to do it, and you were clever, and quick, even when you were half drowned yourself. You fought for me. And you should be the heir to this holt.'

Sedge's mouth dropped open, and the otters fell silent. Silken gazed round defiantly.

'Silken,' Lady Thorn said, blinking. 'My dear one. I suppose no one explained . . . Sedge *was* my heir, but now that you've returned, as the eldest, you would inherit, not him. You will lead the holt when I'm gone.'

'No,' Silken said flatly. 'I won't. I came back to the holt because Sedge asked me to, and because I wanted to see where I was born. I didn't come back to be your heir.'

'You don't have a choice,' Teasel said, her fur wrinkling

into two deep lines between her eyes. 'Heirs are born, that's the way it is. That's the way it's always been. We have the records of the holt to tell us.'

Silken hunched her shoulders. 'Maybe you should think about doing it differently then. Why should everything always have to be the same? Sedge has been brought up to lead the holt, and I haven't. So why don't you let him? Or – or choose someone else, like – like Lily!'

There was a faint squeak in the background, and Lily ducked behind Tormentil. Lady Thorn shook herself, and stood, gazing around at all the otters. 'These are not matters to be settled in one night's talking,' she announced. 'Carry on with your feasting. Be merry tonight, for tomorrow we go back to sweeping the last scraps of flood silt out of our passages and corners.'

Crowfoot bowed to her, one front paw behind his back and the other sweeping low over the ground. 'The holt is lucky to have two such fine cubs,' he murmured, and returned to his place at the table.

Looking at her mother and Teasel, Silken wasn't sure that they agreed.

CHAPTER THREE

Sedge blinked sleepily in the dim light of his bedchamber. *It must be early*, he thought. Silken was still curled deep into her bed of rushes, her tail wrapped around her nose. The celebration had gone on long into the night, but he and Silken had slipped away early with Lily and Tormentil. They had gone to splash and chatter in the shallows a little upstream. Back at the feast there had been too many strange silences, followed by bursts of excited whispering. Too many eyes on them. It was hard to sit and eat while all the gossip went on around them.

'I'd never have thought, would you?'

'Of course, he is Campion's son. His father is a great fighter.'

'But little Sedge . . .'

Tormentil and Lily had been good company, even if every so often Sedge had caught one of them eyeing him sideways – clearly imagining him knocking down the night wolf with a rock. In the end, he had snapped at Lily, 'Stop looking at me like that!'

'Sorry.' She had stared down at her paws, embarrassed. 'I can't help it. I just . . . I can't think of you, picking up a rock like that . . .'

'What would you have done?' Sedge had asked her wearily. 'If it had been Pebble lying there? Or Tormentil? Wouldn't *you* have picked up a rock?'

Lily had lifted her paw to her mouth, nibbling at her claws. 'I don't know,' she had said at last. 'I think I would have been frozen still. Everyone spoke about the night wolf as if she was a monster, that there was something eerie about her. She wasn't like the other creatures of the riverbank, Sedge. Or even the wilder things that come out of the woods. She was . . . more.'

'Why aren't you proud of it?' Tormentil had broken in. 'She was like something out of one of the old tales, wasn't she? That makes you the hero of the story.'

'I was too frightened to be a hero,' Sedge had growled. 'And I don't ever want to do that again. It's not how I want to be remembered.'

Now, in the new morning, he shivered, thinking back to those words. What if killing the night wolf was what he was remembered for always, even after he became lord of the holt? He would be known for something he hated to think about, something that still made him feel sick inside. What if he was expected to do it again?

'Why are you looking like that?' Silken yawned. She wriggled up out of the reeds and peered at him. 'Are you ill? What's wrong?'

'No. Just . . . remembering.'

Silken gave a short little huff, half amused, half sad. 'Maybe don't do that then.'

'We should get up.' Sedge stretched and reached back to nibble a patch of itchy fur. 'Now that the holt's almost back to rights, Ma wants us working with Sorrel again. He's the healer, you know. I expect there are herbs he needs gathering – what we can find under all the mud, anyway.'

Silken popped up out of the reed bedding, looking eager. 'Exploring up and down the banks?'

Sedge nodded. 'It isn't *that* exciting. But I suppose you haven't been able to look around much, with all the repairs we've been doing.'

'Exactly. And that was what I always liked best back at the Stronghold, going out to forage. Gave me a good reason not to go out searching for wood for the dam with the others,' she explained. 'They were all so much better at it than I was, and I didn't understand why I was no good. It meant I could fish without anyone seeing too.'

'We'd better go and get breakfast before Sorrel comes looking for us.' Sedge cast a worried eye over his sister. She was definitely sleeker than she had been when he'd first found her – the good fishing on their journey back up the river had helped with that. She was still thinner than she ought to be, though. The beavers' natural diet of plants and tree bark hadn't been right for an otter, and it had left her thin and undernourished. She still needed feeding up.

Down in the main hall, otters were scattered around the tables eating and discussing the day's work. Breakfast was leftovers from last night's feast, and Sedge gathered up a plate of smoked perch to share with Silken. Bramble hung them in the chimney above the kitchen fire to smoke, and Sedge loved their sharp, rich sweetness.

His mouth was still full of perch when Sorrel appeared next to their table, collecting bags slung about him. He wrinkled his muzzle at their greasy paws. 'You'll be sick,' he said. 'Eating that rich food this early.'

'It's worth it,' Silken replied, swiping the last piece of fish and licking her whiskers.

'Have one of these.' Sorrel passed out the bags. 'Come on. We're going downstream a little way to gather elderflowers.' He cast a sideways look at Silken, clearly remembering that she had been Elderberry, before.

'I like elderflowers,' she murmured. 'They're like the foam you get on the river sometimes. And they smell sweet. What do you use them for?'

Sorrel brightened up at once. 'Ah, now, elderflowers are very good for a cough. We make them into a syrup for that. An excellent remedy for wheezing in the chest. The dried flowers can be steeped in hot water and honey for a sore throat too. My old teacher swore that tufts of fresh elder-blossom stuffed in the ears were just the thing to banish an earache, but looking back, I do wonder if she was teasing me.' He wrinkled his nose thoughtfully, and Sedge tried not to chuckle. Sorrel was known throughout the holt for his kindness, but also for being intensely serious. For someone so clever, he was remarkably good at missing a joke.

Still lecturing them happily about the benefits of elderflowers, Sorrel led the two cubs out of the holt, hopping over the willow tree roots to head downstream. A few minutes later they were clambering in and out of the shallows to reach the straggly clump of elders, cloaked in flat fans of creamy blossom.

'Pick them carefully,' Sorrel instructed as he stood among the frothy whiteness. 'Try not to shake the yellow dust off the flowers, that's where the goodness is.'

'Do we pick all of it?' Silken asked, eyeing the trees.

There was a lot of blossom. She wasn't sure they had enough bags.

'No, no.' Sorrel blinked at her. He seemed to be dazed by the sun and the flowers' sweet smell. 'Only, hmmm, one flower head in four. We need to leave enough to set to berries, you see.' He patted her paw, pointing out the reddish-dark fur that had named her as a tiny cub. 'The berries that were your namesake. We'll be back here in late summer, ready to pick those for syrup too. Bramble and I fight over the harvest.' He snorted.

Late summer. A horrible weight seemed to settle in Sedge's chest as he watched his sister pick the flowers. Would she still be at the holt by berry time? Or would she have travelled on by then, still looking for her place, for somewhere to call home? Silken's angry outburst at the feast had made him wonder. But before she'd snarled at their mother and Teasel, she had been dancing in the water with them all, with Lady River . . .

He sighed, stripping another branch of blossoms. Perhaps that meant nothing – the river went a long way, after all. Silken could still grow to love Lady River many days' journey away. She didn't have to be at Greenriver Holt to be an otter.

He would miss her. Not only because she would be leaving him to inherit their mother's place, but he would miss her for herself. She was gruff and snappish, but she was funny too, and she could be sweet. She seemed to care for him. Then again, she'd had friends at the Stronghold, and she'd been brave enough to leave them behind. Would she abandon him too?

I killed the wolf for you, he wanted to shout. *I'm changed because of it! You can't leave me again!*

He wanted so much to know if she was planning to stay, but he was too afraid to ask her. He went on grimly picking flowers, the sun beating down on his fur.

'Shall we climb the trees, to reach the flowers higher up?' Silken called to Sorrel.

The healer nodded. 'Yes, but be careful. There's not much to an elder, they're stringy sort of things. Be sure the branches can take your weight.'

The two young otters scrambled up the spindly trees, filling the last space in their gathering bags. Sedge was just reaching for a particularly plump and powdery flower-head when he caught a noise above – a familiar rhythmic thumping in the air.

'Do you hear . . .' he started to say to Silken, but she was already clambering higher in the tree, stretching her neck to peer into the sky.

'It's a swan, I'm sure of it!'

'Is it him? Can you tell?'

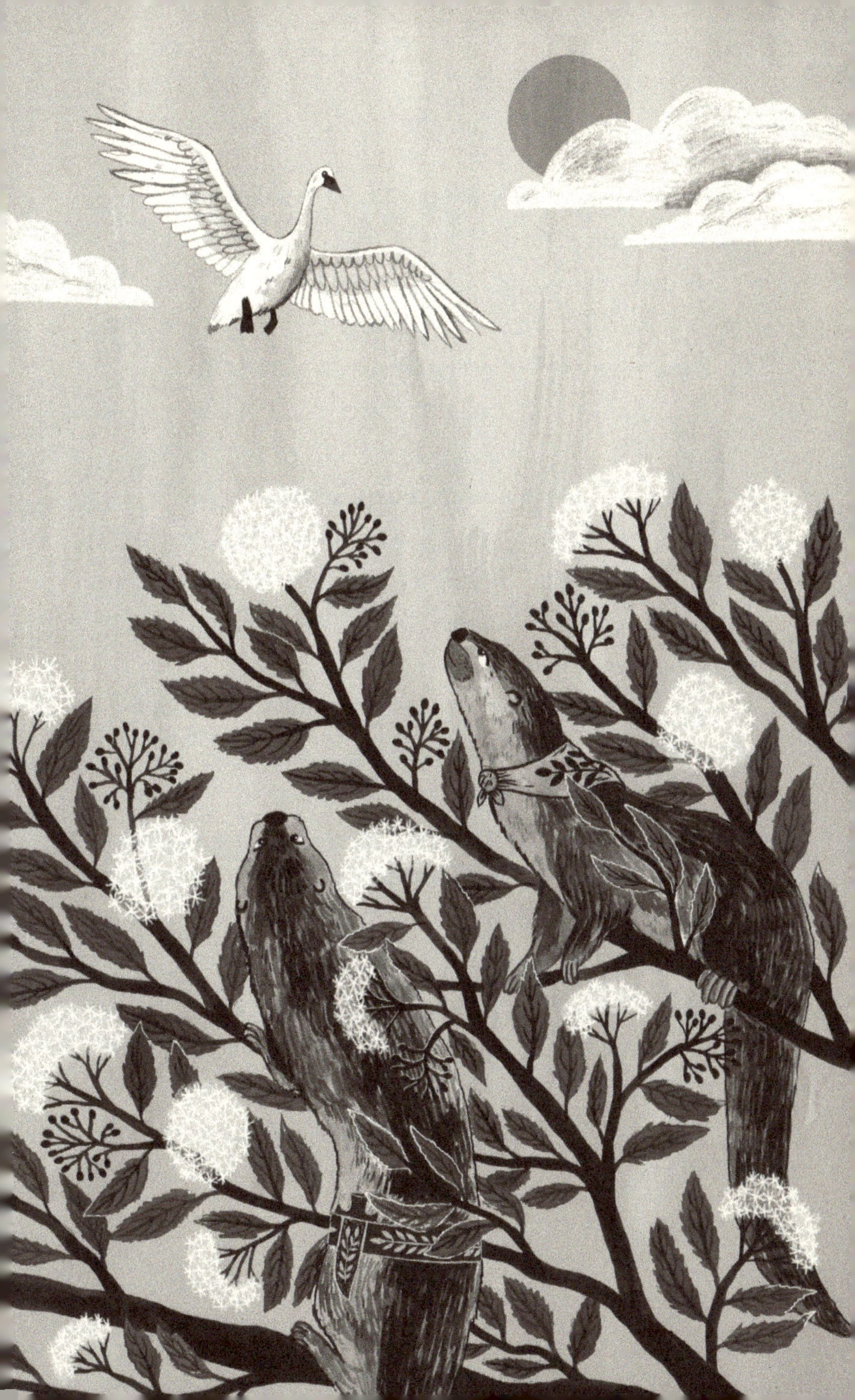

'I don't know.' Silken lifted her front paws from the branch to stretch higher.

Sedge grabbed her. 'You'll fall!' he hissed.

'I wasn't going to,' Silken muttered, but she scrambled down the elder tree, dragging her bag behind her.

'Did you hear that noise?' Sorrel asked. 'Could you see what it was?'

'We think it was a swan,' Sedge explained, grabbing up all the collecting bags. Silken was already hurrying in the direction of the holt. 'Please let us go back, Sorrel. It must have been Vane, the swan who found Silken washed up in his nest, you know.'

'Of course . . .' Sorrel's eyes brightened. 'You think he's on his way to the holt again?'

'He might have brought another message from my father!' Silken called back. Then she stumbled, frowning at them in confusion. 'I mean – I mean from the beaver lodge. Perhaps.'

'Then we must hurry,' Sorrel told her gently. 'Of course you would wish to have word from your old home.'

Silken gave him a grateful nod, and they sped off along the riverbank. It would have been faster to swim, of course, but they couldn't soak the elderflowers.

By the time they'd scrambled through the long grass, the old swan was standing in the clearing by the willow tree, his neck curled graciously down so that Lady Thorn didn't need to look up at him to speak.

'Ah.' Their mother looked pleased. 'I was about to send one of the younger ones to find you.'

'We heard your wingbeats,' Silken told Vane shyly. 'I mean – greetings. I hope your journey wasn't too hard.' She bowed, and Sedge did the same.

Vane nodded back to them. 'I have come to ask for news. There have been rumours, further down the river about two young otters slaying the she-wolf . . .'

Sedge and Silken exchanged a glance. In all the excitement over the letter Vane had brought from Silken's adoptive father during his last visit, they had never told him.

'It was Sedge,' Silken explained. 'He rescued me from her, on our journey back up the river.'

'She's really gone?' A shiver ran through the swan's crisp white feathers, as though the news had shaken him. 'After all this time . . .' he murmured. Then he seemed to remember where he was, drawing up his head and bowing again to Sedge and Silken. 'A great blessing. I shall be glad to carry this news along the river. Glad indeed.'

'Did you bring any news for us?' Sedge asked, since Silken seemed to be hesitating. 'Perhaps another message for my sister?'

'The Master Builder sends you his greetings. He asked me to make sure that you were happy – that you were settling in, now that you've been here a while longer. He sent you this.' He pulled a piece of carefully trimmed birch bark from a loop attached around his leg and held it out to her, his dark eyes glinting as she reached towards his beak.

Silken unfolded the roll of bark, and read the message scratched deeply on to the pale surface.

Dearest one. Be happy. And if you are not, remember that you are always welcome here. Always.

Silken rolled the bark back up and tucked it away inside her scarf to keep it safe. 'It was only saying that he hoped I was well and happy,' she murmured to her mother, feeling that she had to explain.

'I would be glad to carry back any further messages from the holt to the lodge,' Vane went on. Then he added, 'Or I could escort you back down the river, should you wish to return.'

Sedge gasped – he had not expected that. There was a still moment in the clearing, as all the watching otters stared at his sister, waiting for her to answer.

Silken looked between Sedge and her mother, and then at the willow tree. Lady Thorn barely seemed to breathe. Then Silken closed her eyes, and shook her head once. 'No . . . I want to stay here, and learn more about what it is to be an otter.'

The otters sighed, and Sedge was sure that the sound of the river deepened to a chuckle as it flowed over the stones.

'Good news indeed.' The swan nodded and rustled his wing feathers. 'I shall take the chance to explore this stretch of the river before I fly back down towards the Stronghold,' he said, gazing around thoughtfully. 'It's a long time since I've flown this far upstream. I can stop back in to pick up any message you would like to send to Master Grey.'

'I must thank him again for his care of Silken,' Lady Thorn said. 'Each day that she's back with us, I see in her how well she was loved.' She wrinkled her muzzle thoughtfully. 'Otters and beavers have been strangers to one another for too long. Perhaps this is a chance for the holt and the lodge to build an alliance. I must think what to say . . .'

'I should be honoured to carry your message again,' the swan agreed. 'And I can tell the Master Builder that he need not fear the old wolf stalking along the banks and over his dam.'

'Can we offer you food? Somewhere to rest?' Lady Thorn looked a little doubtfully at the entrance to the holt through the hollow tree. 'You are most welcome inside . . .'

The swan gave his harsh chuckle again. 'No hollow trees and underground holds for me, my lady. I sleep on the water.

I'll rest here on the bank a while, before I fly on. Your otters could keep me company. Perhaps they might sing? As I said, your daughter and son sang for me when we met down the river. Their voices are very fine.'

Silken stepped closer, nudging her nose very gently against the fine feathers of the old swan's neck. 'I have a song you might be glad to hear,' she said. 'I made it for your mate – you asked us to remember her.'

'Ah . . .' The swan nibbled at his wing feathers, and Sedge was sure it was to give him a chance to look away. 'My dear Quill. She would have been so curious about this journey up the river. Please, sing your song for me.' He padded to the edge of the bank and settled himself in the shallow water between the willow tree roots.

Silken beckoned Sedge closer, and then her friends among the younger otters, Tormentil and Lily, as well as the little ones Willow and Marigold. They gathered on the bank around the swan, humming gently as Silken closed her eyes. Sedge stood close to his sister's side, sure that he could hear her heart hammering as she began to sing.

When the mist lies on the river,
I see you.
Or when the dawn breaks cold and grey.

When the sun shines on the water,
Then I see you.
And when the wind sighs in the trees.

When the shadows grow at evening,
It's then I see you.
Whenever night is drawing in.

When a swan flies down the river,
I see not them, but only you.
And my heart tears deep inside.

It was hard to listen to the words, even harder to watch the old swan as he heard them. After the first few lines, Sedge closed his eyes too. The harmony of the otter voices seemed almost too sweet as they sang Vane's memory and sadness back to him.

They let the words die away at the end. Sedge stood silently on the bank, feeling his sister droop against his shoulder, hearing her soft breathing. The swan was facing out towards the water now, gazing downstream towards his nesting site. The great flood last spring had swept his mate away, on the same day it had cast Silken up half drowned in her nest. Then he looked back at them. 'You spoke for me,' he said, so softly that they could hardly hear him above the lapping water.

Sedge felt Silken press her paw against his own. 'For all of us who've gone on, and left someone behind,' she whispered.

That first letter that Vane had brought to the holt had been addressed formally to Silken's mother, of course, but Lady Thorn had given it to Silken to read. She must have seen her daughter tracing the spidery words with one claw, over and over. That evening, the fragile curl of pale bark had appeared on the stone shelf in Sedge and Silken's chamber, carefully stored in a little wooden box. Silken had left the lodge with nothing, and the message from her old home was a treasure.

Our daughter, Master Grey had called her in that letter. Silken had watched her mother read it, and seen the darkness in her eyes. It seemed that Lady Thorn had accepted that she would always have to share her eldest cub, but it hurt her. It made the present of the message in its tiny box even more generous.

And now, *Dearest one*. He missed her. He did. Even though she'd always felt that she puzzled and disappointed him, that she was somehow lacking. She tucked the second message safely away in the little box with the first, knowing that she would read it again and again.

Sedge was unsure about the messages, Silken could see that. His eyes went to the wooden box often when they were curling up to sleep. He was still worried that she would decide to go back, Silken thought. She had been speaking the truth when she told the old swan that she wanted to stay and learn to be an otter – she certainly didn't want to go back to not properly belonging at the Stronghold.

It was only that she missed them too – and it was so good to know that she hadn't been forgotten.

The otters watched Vane take off from the water the next morning, launching himself above the trees with a harsh yawp of excitement. He seemed younger, Silken thought. The journey up the river had put new life into him. He promised that he would visit again on his way back, to pick up Lady Thorn's message and pass on the news and gossip from further up towards the mountains. The otters expected him in a week or so, perhaps a bit longer if he found any old comrades to stop with.

Vane was back far sooner. Two days after he had left, they heard his wingbeats above the trees, but they sounded halting and uneven, as though the old swan could hardly keep himself aloft. He struggled and splashed down into the river before the holt, scattering the littlest otters, who'd been playing around the willow tree roots. His neck drooped and one of his wings was held out oddly to the side, dragging in the water.

Silken launched herself into the river, speeding towards him, and Sedge hurried after her. 'What happened?' she gasped, nudging gently at Vane's neck. The tiny white feathers were ruffled and streaked with blood.

The swan hissed faintly, rearing back as though he hadn't seen the otters coming. He was dazed, Silken realised. Almost fainting. 'Sedge, you'd better find Sorrel!' she said urgently. 'Vane's injured. He's bleeding!'

She coaxed the swan to the water's edge, chittering worriedly as he stumbled out on to the willow tree roots, and she saw the extent of his injuries. There was a long gash streaking blood down the side of his neck, but it was his left wing that really frightened her. She wasn't sure how he'd managed to fly at all. Great chunks of white feathers had been torn away, and the swan was trailing it behind him, as though it hurt too much to bear the weight.

Sorrel darted out of the holt with a satchel of healer's remedies, and Sedge followed, carrying bandages.

'What did this to you?' Sorrel murmured, teasing out the crumpled feathers with gentle paws. 'Have you been . . . attacked?'

'Foxes . . .' Vane groaned, and Sorrel let out a shocked hiss. Then he looked round at Silken. 'Get your mother,' he said to her. 'Tell her it's urgent. Tell her . . . what Vane said. And Sedge, you head along the bank to that patch of wild garlic by the old oak tree. We need to make a poultice of the leaves to put on these wounds. Bites are dangerous; they can fester.'

Lady Thorn was in the kitchens with Bramble inspecting the holt stores while the cook grumbled about the damage the flood had done to his shelves of crocks and jars. 'Years' worth,' he was muttering, as Silken tumbled in. 'All that waste! What d'you want, child? You look like the wolf's behind you!'

'Ma, we need you,' Silken gabbled. 'Vane's back, and he's hurt. He says it was foxes!'

There was a moment of still silence in the kitchen, then Lady Thorn shot out of the back door, galloping along the bank towards the little knot of worried otters who were watching Sorrel work.

Sorrel had drawn Vane in to the side of the bank, resting

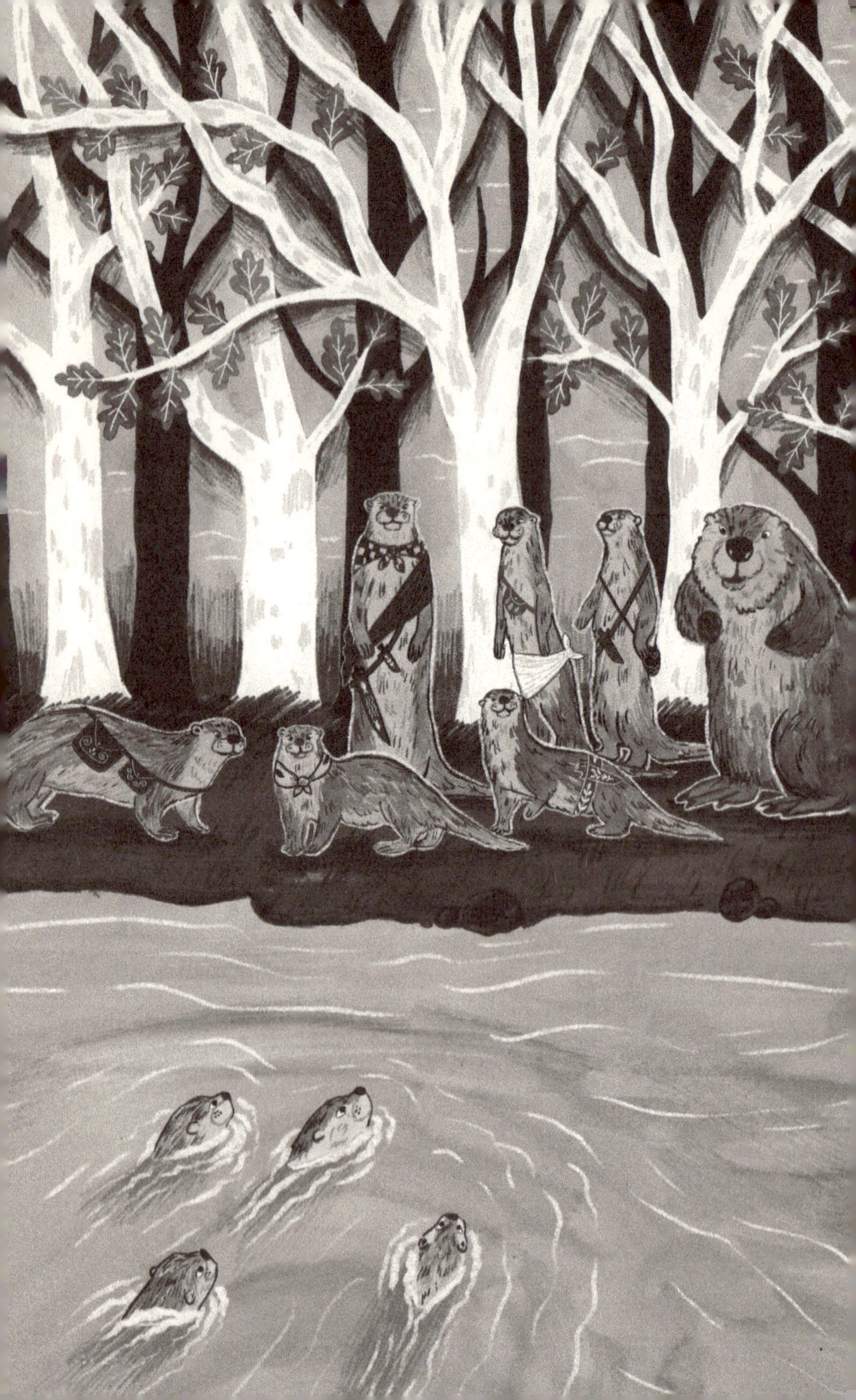

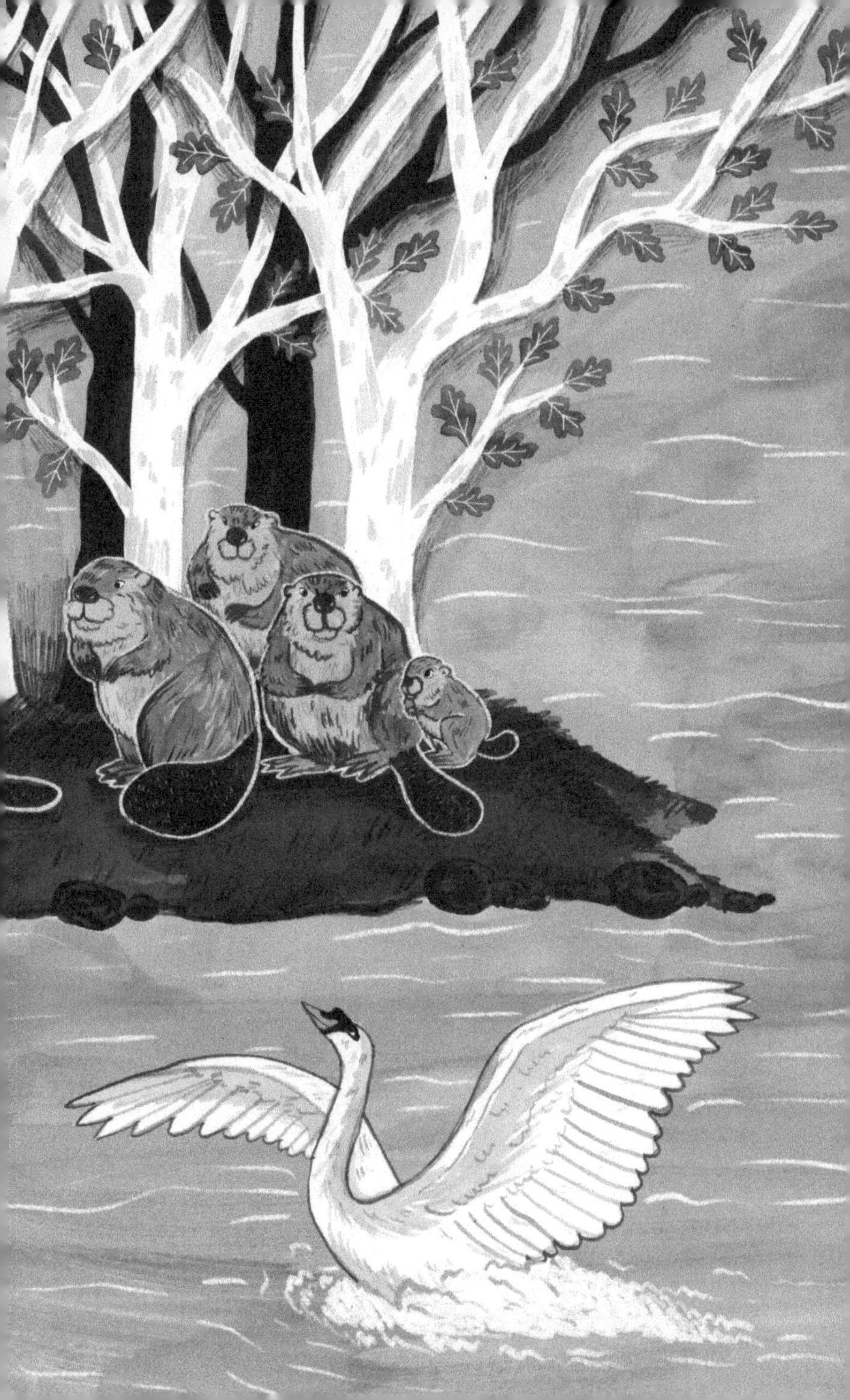

him in a hollow between two knotted tree roots. The swan was slumped over with his neck drooping and his battered wing stretched out for the healer to examine. Sorrel was still prodding at the feathers and muttering, while Sedge pounded a stone bowl full of wild garlic leaves with a smooth, fat pebble.

'Is it done? Did you mix in the honey?' Sorrel peered over, and poked a claw into the greenish pulp. 'Good. Now, help me plaster it on over the wound . . .' He glanced round at Lady Thorn and Silken. 'You can talk to him,' he murmured. 'He could do with the distraction while we're dressing this.'

The old swan uncurled his neck a little, lifting his head to look at them all. 'I heard that. Just what are you covering my feathers in?' he added, catching the pungent scent of the garlic leaves.

'Garlic and honey,' Sorrel explained soothingly. 'Both very good for drawing any nastiness out of a bite wound. Tell Lady Thorn what happened to you.'

Vane sighed. 'I fell in with bad company . . . Don't look at me like that,' he added grumpily. 'I'm in pain here, I'm allowed to joke.' He shivered. 'I tried to roost overnight just downstream from a ravening band of foxes, that's what happened.'

'Where were they?' Lady Thorn demanded. 'I didn't know

there were any foxes closer than the mountains. That's . . . well, half a river away from here.'

'They were closer than that,' Vane said. 'Not a lot closer. But closer than they have been. I heard a lot of gossip on my way up the river. Spoke to a kingfisher, and a few geese. Even a falcon. They all said the same. The river changed its path up in the mountains when it flooded earlier in the spring. There was so much water that there was nowhere for it to go, so it scoured out a new path. Everything in its way just isn't there any more.' He sucked in a sharp breath as Sorrel laid another layer of green paste on his injured wing. 'Careful there! Feathers are fragile.'

Sorrel murmured something apologetic, and the swan shivered the feathers on his other wing and went on. 'I wonder if the foxes' den was one of the things in the way. Certainly they had baggage with them. Not a lot, just bundles, as if they'd had to escape in a hurry, or had gone back to salvage what they could before they abandoned their den.'

Lady Thorn looked aghast. 'You think they're travelling downriver to look for a new home?'

Vane hesitated. Eventually, he nodded. 'They could be.'

CHAPTER FOUR

'Teasel . . .' Silken looked back along the fallen tree at the edge of the bank, eyeing the grizzled old otter. She was still nervous about speaking to her. 'The news the swan brought yesterday, about the foxes. Why is everyone so terrified of them? What would happen if they came down as far as the holt?'

It was hard to return to duties and tidying and lessons after all the excitement of Vane's arrival and the full-scale panic that his news had caused, but Teasel had marched them up the bank that morning nonetheless to search for spots that had been weakened by the flood. Despite Silken refusing to be acknowledged as the holt's heir, Teasel and Thorn seemed to think that both the young otters needed educating in the heir's responsibilities.

Sorrel had been pleased with the swan's recovery that morning, but he had flatly refused to let Vane fly back down the river yet. 'Of course you can't!' he'd snapped, horrified at the suggestion. 'You need to rest and heal! I still don't know how you managed to get back to us with your wing in that state. Any more exertion could mean permanent damage!'

Sorrel was usually so gentle that his sharp words had all the otters scurrying to get out of his way. Even the huge swan had looked a little daunted, and he'd consented to stay at the holt and be nursed back to health.

Now Teasel sniffed disgustedly at Silken's question. 'Foxes,' she muttered, 'are vermin.'

Sedge's stubby whiskers twitched. 'You told me that beavers were fierce and cruel,' he pointed out. 'And they can't be that bad, since they took Silken in, even if they are a bit odd. I didn't mean to be rude,' he added quickly, as Silken glared at him. 'What I'm saying is, Greenriver otters have always kept ourselves to ourselves, haven't we?'

'Exactly!' Silken nodded, grateful that he'd understood. 'That's what I was thinking. Perhaps foxes aren't as bad as we think they are?'

'Did you not see what they did to Vane?' Teasel scowled at her.

'Yes, of course . . . But . . . I don't know, maybe they thought he was attacking them? I mean, we've never met any foxes. It might be that we just don't understand them.'

'I have met them,' Teasel growled, 'and I never want to again.'

'What are they like?' Silken demanded eagerly.

'You're supposed to be inspecting the riverbank,' Teasel pointed out. 'Not getting me nattering on about foxes.'

With a sigh, Sedge and Silken turned back to the river. 'We need to peg rush netting down here,' Sedge told her after a moment, hanging almost upside down off the tree trunk to examine the crumbling earth among the roots. 'The tree was shoring this part of the bank up, I think. Look at all that silt in the water. It's giving way. The current's going to carry the trunk off down the river sooner or later, I'd say. What do you think, Silken?'

Even though she'd been a most disappointing builder compared to the other young beavers, Silken had still shared their training. 'Yes, the trunk won't last much longer. It's a pity we can't float it away ourselves,' she said thoughtfully. 'We could set it up by the holt, use it to turn the flow of the river, and fend away any more flood surges.'

'Beavers,' Teasel muttered. 'Such strangeness. Thinking you can alter Lady River's plans . . .' But she eyed the tree trunk thoughtfully.

'We might as well go and pick the rushes from that clump on the other side of the river,' said Sedge, 'and weave it now since we're here. While we're at it you can tell us all about foxes.'

'Yeah,' agreed Silken. 'It's part of the holt-lore, isn't it? I'm supposed to learn all that. Besides, if they're such a threat to the holt, we should know about them!'

Teasel sighed. 'Go and gather your reeds then. Long ones, mind, good and strong.'

Silken dived off the tree trunk and Sedge followed, and they arrowed through the water to the reeds, biting free great bunches of stems to lay out in piles along the bank. Then they settled on the grass, knotting the reeds together into a fine mesh, while Teasel tapped her claws together thoughtfully.

'Sedge will tell you,' she began, looking at Silken, 'that I never had anything good to say about beavers. Which was wrong of me. Perhaps,' she added.

'If it helps, beavers don't have anything good to say about otters either,' Silken told her, biting off the long end of a reed stem. 'I grew up being told that otters wanted to make me into a little fur hat.'

Sedge snorted, and even Teasel looked amused. But then her expression grew serious. 'We spun most of those tales out of nothing, looking back. Your foster-father was the first beaver I'd ever seen, gazing at us across the river when he came to make sure you were all right. All I could think when I saw him was, *That's what I've been so afraid of?*'

Silken laid down her bundle of reeds. 'I know,' she said. 'But then imagine finding out that all along, you *were* the very thing you'd been afraid of. I think . . . I think beavers are more scared of otters than you are of them. Beavers don't hunt. They're a peaceable sort of creature. They build things. Otters always seemed wild and strange and frightening. It was very brave of my father – my foster-father – to follow me up the river.'

'Hmmm.' Teasel nodded, and picked up the edge of the net that Sedge and Silken had begun to weave. She tugged at the knots. 'It needs to be tighter,' she said. 'Knot the stems closer together. Yes, perhaps we were wrong about beavers. Foxes, now, that's a whole different story. I know them, all too well.' She was silent then, and the two young otters watched her, transfixed.

'Are they – are they like the wolf?' Silken asked at last. Foxes and wolves were related, or so she'd heard.

'Mmm. Not far off,' Teasel agreed. 'Smaller, of course. Not that much larger than an otter. But almost as vicious as the old wolf was. They hunt in packs too, some of them. A murderous gang of thieves. Foxes hunt for the joy of it, you see. Like the wolf. They can't resist the instinct – and it doesn't stop when they kill.' She gave a shudder. 'They go into a frenzy. Jumping about, spitting feathers, shaking their prey even after death. And then they just abandon what they don't need and leave it all to rot.'

Sedge leaned forward. 'Teasel, have you *seen* foxes doing those things? That doesn't sound just like stories. Were there foxes close to the holt before?' He glanced sideways, as if they might find foxes creeping up on them all of a sudden.

'No. Not here.'

'You've travelled somewhere else?' Silken sat up, staring curiously at Teasel, and Sedge dropped the net in surprise.

'I didn't know you'd left the holt!'

'I travelled with the raft otters for a summer, long ago. When I wasn't much older than you.' Teasel gazed off into the middle of the river, remembering. 'It was something that cubs often did, in those days. It was good experience, part of our growing up.'

'Why don't we do that now?' Sedge asked jealously. Going on a journey down the river with his father's people sounded so exciting.

Teasel seemed to shrink, huddling herself towards the bank. 'It was given up,' she said. 'Too dangerous.'

The two cubs watched her, waiting for more. At last she sighed, and went on. 'The holt stopped sending its cubs out when one cub didn't come back. It was that same summer that I travelled with the raft otters – the cub's name was Blossom. She and I were so excited to journey together. They had promised us that we could go all the way down the river to the sea. But we camped on the riverbank one night, and in the morning Blossom had disappeared. There was nothing left of her, just scratched earth and torn-up grasses where she'd been sleeping.' Teasel's eyes thinned. 'We set out to track her, and we found them later that morning, in the woods. Two foxes and Blossom.' Her voice dropped so low that Sedge and Silken could hardly hear her next words. 'They'd killed her. And they knew we'd come after them. The way they looked at us, with such sneering glee . . .'

'Why?' Silken whispered, horrified.

'Because they were foxes,' Teasel told her grimly.

'But – maybe they were just bad foxes?' Sedge suggested helplessly. 'And not all foxes are like that.'

'Foxes are all the same.'

Silken's voice shook as she asked, 'What did you do?'

'The large fox hissed at us – and then they both disappeared into the trees. They seemed to melt away into the shadows.' Teasel shuddered. 'They left Blossom's body. We tried to revive her, but of course it was no good. The foxes were long gone then. None of us had the heart or the strength to go after them. So we laid Blossom on a bed of branches in the middle of the raft, and poled her back to the holt.' Teasel shook her head, and Silken thought she looked older all of a sudden. 'I've never left the holt since.'

'I'm sorry,' Sedge whispered.

'And now there are foxes coming down the river,' Teasel growled. 'We need to guard our cubs. You young ones mustn't be out alone. I'll talk to your mother about it.'

'We don't know that the foxes will come anywhere near us, though,' Silken pointed out. She had only just got to the holt, and she'd hardly had a chance to explore, what with all the work they'd had to do clearing up after the flood. After their adventures travelling up the river from the lodge, she didn't want to be fussed over like some tiny cub.

'We won't be risking anything,' Teasel said flatly. 'Never go out alone, you hear me? I know you think it was a long time ago, and those foxes who took Blossom were just a couple of bad seeds. And you've both travelled alone before, and I'm just fussing and forgetting that you fought and killed a wolf, so what's a band of foxes to that?'

Silken looked embarrassed. 'I wasn't thinking *exactly* that . . .'

'You're right, of course.' Teasel reached out to lay her greying paw on Silken's. 'But I wake up in the middle of the night still and see those foxes. Those pale eyes staring back at me. The grin, all those teeth. The way Blossom hung in their paws, so limp . . . I'll never forget.' She shook herself. 'The raft otters go travelling and trading, and I wish them well. But we stay with our own kind for a reason.'

Sedge gnawed on a claw, listening to the argument snapping back and forth across the hall. Since Vane and his news had arrived, the otters had been gathering in terrified clumps to talk about the foxes. Teasel's worry made sense, given her story about poor Blossom – but she wasn't the only one panicking about where the foxes might head for next. Last night at dinner there had been frightened muttering. Tonight, everyone had digested the news and spent the whole day talking about it. The hall was in uproar. What were the foxes doing? Would they come this far down the river? Would they want to steal the holt? Should the otters set off upriver at once to fight them? Or was it just a silly rumour, and who on the river would listen to birds, anyway?

'Do *you* think the foxes might want to live here?' Silken whispered to him. 'Is Teasel right to be so worried?'

Sedge turned to her, his muzzle wrinkling. 'How would

we know? I think Teasel's the only otter in the holt who's *met* a fox.'

'Vane's met one, and it mauled him.'

Sedge turned a little, looking out of the holt entrance towards the river, where Vane was curled among the willow roots, his head tucked under his wing. Sorrel was out there with him keeping him company. He was probably telling the old swan all about his latest way of preserving angelica root, or getting Vane to show him how feathers fitted together. Sorrel wanted to know everything, and he adored explaining it to everyone else. But his patients liked it – his long lectures were soothing, and made them feel as though Sorrel knew what he was doing, even when they were half asleep.

'He's sleeping a lot.'

'Is that bad?'

Sedge sighed. 'I'm not sure. Sleep's good for healing – he needs to rest. Or it could mean that his body's struggling to mend. He's old, Silken.'

'He's strong though,' Silken argued. 'All those trips up and down the river. He can fly for days.'

Sedge nodded. 'I still can't believe he flew back here with his wing so torn up. He was desperate to warn us that the foxes were coming. I suppose we should be listening to him, even if – even if we're afraid to.'

'Let's go and listen then,' Silken suggested. Sedge nodded, wriggling off the bench, and the pair of them ducked discreetly away into the shadows, making for one of the holt's side doors.

Outside, the river glowed orange in the sunset light, casting an eerie glare over Vane's white feathers. The two cubs could hear the slow stream of Sorrel's gentle chatter. The swan seemed to be listening, even though his eyes were closed. He grunted every so often, and once they heard a soft chuckling sound.

'What are you two lurking over there for?' the swan grumbled, gracefully untwisting his neck to peer at them both.

'We came to talk to you,' Silken explained, and she bobbed her head to the healer too. 'Good evening, Sorrel.'

'Everyone's arguing in there,' Sedge added. 'We didn't know who to believe. So we came to ask you, instead. Since you were the one who actually met the foxes.'

Vane snorted. 'Hardly. I caught sight of their camp, and then I saw one of the beasts, and only while he was savaging my wing.'

Silken gave a disappointed sigh. 'So you didn't talk to them at all?'

'I did not.' Vane glared down at them, and then sighed too. 'I apologise for not interrogating the fox about his troop's evil plans while I was fighting him off.'

'We didn't mean it like that.' Sedge twisted his paws together, looking apologetic. 'It's just, no one really knows what's happening, do they? What the foxes are actually like!'

'They are clearly savage,' Sorrel put in. 'Vane's wounds show that. But you're right, we don't know what their motives are. Or how far down the river they mean to travel.'

'I've flown over their old den before, you know.' Vane nodded to himself. 'It was under a hollow tree. Much like your holt, in some ways. They've lived there as long as anyone on the river can remember. If they're on their way down the river searching for a new home, Greenriver Holt would catch their eye.'

'But – but it's ours!' Sedge cried. 'They can't just take our home.'

'Perhaps you'd say a fox can't just leap on an old swan minding his business in a patch of soggy reeds either?' Vane snapped. 'But he did.'

'What does your mother think of all this?' Sorrel asked.

Sedge and Silken exchanged a glance, and Silken shrugged. 'You say. You know her better.'

'She's . . . tired,' Sedge admitted at last. 'I think she's still so worn out after the flood, and all those times she tried to sing the waters down without it working. I don't think she wants to know about the foxes. She's closed her ears, as if she were under the water.' He squirmed uncomfortably, not wanting to meet Sorrel's eyes. He almost wanted the healer to tell him off for saying something so stupid.

But Sorrel only nodded. 'You weren't here to see her miss you either,' he pointed out. 'On top of her grieving for your sister. She lost both her cubs, for a while. I was quite worried about her.'

Sedge hung his head. 'I left for a good reason. I brought Silken back.'

'And we thank the river for that, every day,' Sorrel agreed. 'Just don't be too quick to judge Lady Thorn. The flood, the foxes . . . there's a lot she's having to deal with.'

Silken twitched, her whiskers flickering. 'Someone's coming,' she murmured. 'Hush.'

'I thought I might find you two out here.' Lady Thorn emerged out of the shadows with Teasel lumbering after her, sniffing suspiciously at the evening breeze.

Vane lowered his head in a respectful nod. 'We were talking of the foxes.'

'Yes . . . There's much to discuss.' Lady Thorn sighed.

'We should send a scouting party up the river at once,' Teasel growled. 'We need to find out what they're after. If we leave it much longer we'll wake up to find foxes in our hall eating our breakfast.'

'They're still far away,' Lady Thorn said wearily, as if she'd said it many times before. 'Remember they don't swim – or fly.' Here she nodded politely to Vane.

Vane straightened up with a faint groan. 'With respect, Lady, you're right that they don't swim. They run instead, and they can take a straight path, same as I can. They don't need to follow the bends and turns of the river, like an otter. If they ford across where it's shallow, they can cut out a hefty portion of the journey.'

Sedge saw his mother's shoulders sag still further. 'Yes . . . yes, I suppose.'

'Do you really think they want to take our holt?' Silken asked, looking round at them all.

'I think they're looking for a new home of their own,' Lady Thorn murmured reluctantly, with a glance at Teasel. 'Who knows where they'll find it? It could be here.' She took a deeper breath and dragged herself upright. 'We must face that. I must—'

'We should warn the Stronghold,' Silken said abruptly.

Lady Thorn blinked, and Sedge gave his sister a surprised look.

'What for?' Teasel demanded. 'We've enough to worry about.'

'The foxes could cut straight past us and head further

downstream. The river's wider and deeper there, and the woods are more open. Easier hunting . . . They might like a home there better. The beavers won't know about the danger. It's our duty to warn them!'

Teasel sniffed. '*Your* duty is to guard your holt and help your mother, since this should be your holt one day.'

'I told you—' Silken burst out angrily, but Lady Thorn interrupted her, grimacing at Teasel.

'Now isn't the time to discuss that.'

So they still hoped to persuade her, then. Sedge felt something twist inside him, and he wasn't sure if it was hope or disappointment. He didn't even know what he wanted any more.

Vane stretched out his injured wing, wincing. 'In a day or two . . .'

Sorrel glared at him. 'You're going nowhere.'

'But she's right. The lodge must be warned—'

'Do you ever want it to heal?' Sorrel snapped.

'I didn't mean you needed to go,' Silken told the swan gently.

'So you want us to send otters down the river on some useless errand now, when we're about to be under attack.' Teasel huffed in disgust. 'We should be able to expect *some* loyalty to the holt from you, surely.'

'But we were going to try to build an alliance,' Sedge

argued, seeing his sister flinch at the harsh words. It was cruel of Teasel to play on Silken's fear of not fitting in with her true family. 'You wrote to the beavers, Ma! You were going to send another message too.'

Lady Thorn lifted her paws, rubbing at the greying fur around her eyes. 'I did,' she said tiredly. 'Teasel. We need a meeting of the holt. We'll gather out here, so our guest can be part of the discussion. The time for whispers and rumour and panic is gone. We must make a plan.'

'If we're going to have to fight off the foxes, surely we need all the help we can get!' Sorrel said, looking round at the crowd of otters.

Lady Thorn nodded reluctantly at him to continue.

'We should send messengers to the Stronghold at once. If we send them a warning, we can ask for their help at the same time. The lady of the holt has already had friendly words from them.'

'That doesn't mean they'll be sending beavers up here to fight for us,' scoffed one of the holt guards. 'Friendly words are all very well, but they mean nothing when it comes to a scrap.'

'Excuse me breaking into your meeting.' Vane poked his neck out, sending several otters scuttling back. 'This won't be a *scrap*. If the foxes are indeed heading downstream to steal themselves a home – which I suspect they are – then what you're looking at is a full-scale attack, by a band of vicious and ruthless hunters. Not a fun wrestling match. You need allies.'

'May I speak?'

Silken peered at the otter who'd just stood up. She was familiar somehow, but Silken wasn't sure why. She didn't remember meeting her. Then the otter brushed a paw over her whiskers, as though she was a little nervous, and Silken recognised the gesture. The otter looked like Lily – and yes, there was Lily behind her, her expression troubled. Lily's brother Pebble was there too, nodding eagerly as his mother went on, 'Surely we need no beavers to fight for us. Our holt stands for itself, it always has! If we beg for beavers to come upriver and help us, don't you see what will happen next?' She cast around pleadingly at the crowd of otters. 'They'll be sending messages begging for us to come and help *them*!'

'What's so wrong about that?' Silken whispered to Sedge. 'It sounds sensible to me. They help us and we help them back.'

Silken scanned the crowd. Other otters were frowning, but there were a few uncertain nods.

'We don't know these creatures,' another otter called out. 'Can we even trust them?'

'They raised my daughter,' Lady Thorn said angrily, and several otters clapped their paws together. 'Don't we owe them at least a warning, Celandine? Even if they don't decide to come upriver and fight for us? Surely they deserve that favour?'

Lily's mother shook her head. 'If it were my cub, I'm sure I'd say the same. But – as the lady of the holt, you should be caring for all our cubs! This isn't just about Elderberry.'

Silken sucked in a breath, and she heard Sedge mutter beside her. None of the otters had called her by her old name before.

'My daughter's name is Silken now,' Lady Thorn said coldly.

Celandine looked over at Silken and shook her head again, and a little rustle of whispering ran round the gathered otters. Silken hunched her shoulders over, trying to make herself small. It was just what she used to do at the Stronghold, she realised miserably, except then she had been trying to make herself round and bunchy, like a beaver.

'That's not an otter name. Elderberry is an otter. She

should forget her time with the beavers. Lady River claimed her! She belongs here, with us.'

'Of course she does. But she grew up as Silken, and I won't force her to change that now.' Lady Thorn shook her head. 'Let's leave the matter of sending messages to the Stronghold for now – we can't be distracted from what's most urgent. We must guard the holt against the foxes. Tomorrow we'll send a scouting party up the river to watch for them.'

The whispering rose to a hum of approval now, and otters pressed forward to volunteer. Lady Thorn nodded gratefully, clasping paws with them all, and Silken turned to Sedge, her eyes wide with anger. 'It's not a distraction, warning my father! How can she say that?'

Sedge shrugged uncomfortably. 'It's more important now to find out what's actually happening.'

Silken turned and plunged away from the crowd of otters, flinging herself into the water. There was a scuffle in the grass, and then a splash as Sedge went after her.

'Silken, come back! I only meant that there's no point going all the way down the river to warn the lodge if we don't even know what we're warning them about!'

Silken stopped, the water swirling around her. 'Is that really what you meant?'

'Yes! Truly, Silken. And it's the same for Ma. She does want to warn the beavers. You know how grateful she is to your foster-father for keeping you safe. I think she'd do anything for him.'

'But then why won't she?'

'Only because she can't, don't you see? Not yet. She has to bring us all together with her. It takes time. It's a struggle, persuading all the holt. It means arguing, and compromise – and sometimes you don't like what you have to do to make everyone agree.' Sedge wrung his paws together, the way he did whenever he was upset. It annoyed Silken every time, and she growled at him, suddenly furious.

'Thorn's supposed to be the lady of the holt. She's in charge, isn't she? She can do whatever she likes! I don't see why you're sticking up for her! None of you care what happens to my real family.'

'Silken!' Sedge pulled back from her, obviously shocked.

'Get away from me!'

'Fine then!' he snapped. 'I will, if that's what you want. Why don't you just go back to the Stronghold if you're so worried about the beavers?' He dived away under the surface of the water, leaving Silken staring at the stream of bubbles rising off his coat, wondering why she had ever come back.

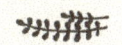

She was still there. At least she hadn't actually taken him at his word and gone back to the lodge. Sedge peered at his sister through the darkness, wondering if she was actually asleep, or just pretending. The curl of her back seemed very stiff.

He slowed his breathing again, trying to sound as though he was asleep himself. He certainly didn't want her thinking that he was awake and worrying about her. *She* was the one who was being unreasonable! How could she say that the beavers were her real family? She'd hated it at the lodge – she had been lonely, and out of place.

But he'd told her to go back there. Sedge squirmed miserably in his bed of reeds, wishing he could unsay the words. Then he froze, hearing a rustle, followed by the stealthy padding of paws over the dirt floor. Where was she going?

Sedge bounced up out of the reeds with a sharp yelp.

'Sssshhh!' Silken hissed at him. 'You'll wake our mother. Go back to sleep.'

Sedge looked at the doorway to their mother's chamber, which joined on to theirs. 'I won't! What are you doing?'

'What you told me to do.' She hesitated in the opening of the chamber. 'Someone has to warn them, Sedge. I – I didn't really mean that they were my real family. But my father tried to be. He did his best. I can't abandon them now.'

'I'm coming with you then.'

Silken shook her head. 'You can't. It would mean leaving our mother alone again. You can't do that to her, Sedge. You told me how much it aged her when you left before.'

'Well, I'm not letting you set off downriver on your own! Ma would be more worried about that than she would about both of us going.'

'He's right.'

Both cubs jumped, and turned slowly to see a patch of thicker darkness across the chamber – their mother, leaning against the door.

'I would rather you go together,' Lady Thorn said gently.

'You want us to go?' Silken sounded confused.

There was a sigh in the darkness. 'Teasel and Celandine were wrong to say that your only loyalty should be to us. It makes me proud that you still want to protect your friends at the beaver lodge. And I think you're right, that we need all the allies we can get. I don't know if the beavers will want to fight for us, but we have to ask. And I'd rather you were together than one of you travel alone.' Lady Thorn stepped forward, gripping their paws in hers so tightly. 'You will watch out for each other? You promise me that you'll be careful?'

'We will.' Silken pulled closer, leaning against her mother's shoulder. 'Thank you.'

'I must send you with a gift for your foster-father, Silken,' Lady Thorn murmured into her fur. 'And our message. Get yourselves ready to leave, my dear ones. I'll find Teasel – she'll know what we have put away, something that you can take as a gesture of friendship to the lodge.' She nuzzled Silken's whiskers again, and then pulled gently away, hurrying out into the passage to look for Teasel.

'We're really going,' Silken whispered.

Sedge felt around the little shelf for a tinder box and lit the lamp. 'We are.' He grinned at her, showing all his teeth in a little chuckle of excitement. 'We'd better hurry – before Ma changes her mind. Let's go down to the kitchens and see if there's any leftovers from dinner we can take with us.'

Bramble was still pottering around the kitchen by the light of the dying fire, humming a quiet tune to himself as he stacked up platters and set cups on the shelves. 'After a late snack, are we?' he asked as they peered round the doorway.

'We're going downriver,' Sedge told him, half proud, half anxious. What if Bramble was one of those who thought otters should be for otters alone?

'Ah, I wondered.' Bramble nodded. 'You'll need rations. Those beavers never fed my little Silken properly. Here.' He shoved a waterproofed cloth bag into Sedge's paws, and started to search among his shelves. 'Now, there are honey cakes here.

Dried perch too. A little of that trout left, I seem to remember. It's not for now!' he added sharply, as Sedge sniffed curiously at one of the little parcels. 'Tuck it all away neatly. Greedy little cubs . . .'

Sedge rolled his eyes at Silken, but he didn't really mind Bramble fussing. These were all the best treats.

'There.' Bramble said, handing them a last package. 'You're not to open that until at least dawn tomorrow. Eat the trout up for your breakfast, it'll not last. Safe journey . . .'

'We'll see you soon,' Sedge promised, as they scurried away down the passage to the front of the holt, where their mother and Teasel were waiting, their lamp casting a golden light on to the water.

'There you are.' Teasel sniffed disapprovingly, but she didn't say anything else about loyalty to the holt. 'Bramble gave you supplies then? Good. Here.' She held out a small waxed cloth pouch to Silken. 'For Master Grey. A gift from the holt.'

'To thank him for taking care of you,' Lady Thorn explained. 'Open it.'

Sedge watched Silken's shaking paws as she nervously undid the buttons that held the pouch closed and lifted out a tiny parcel wrapped in soft woven reeds. Inside was a glowing mussel shell – like the one the holt used for ceremonies, the one that Sedge had dropped in the river all that time before.

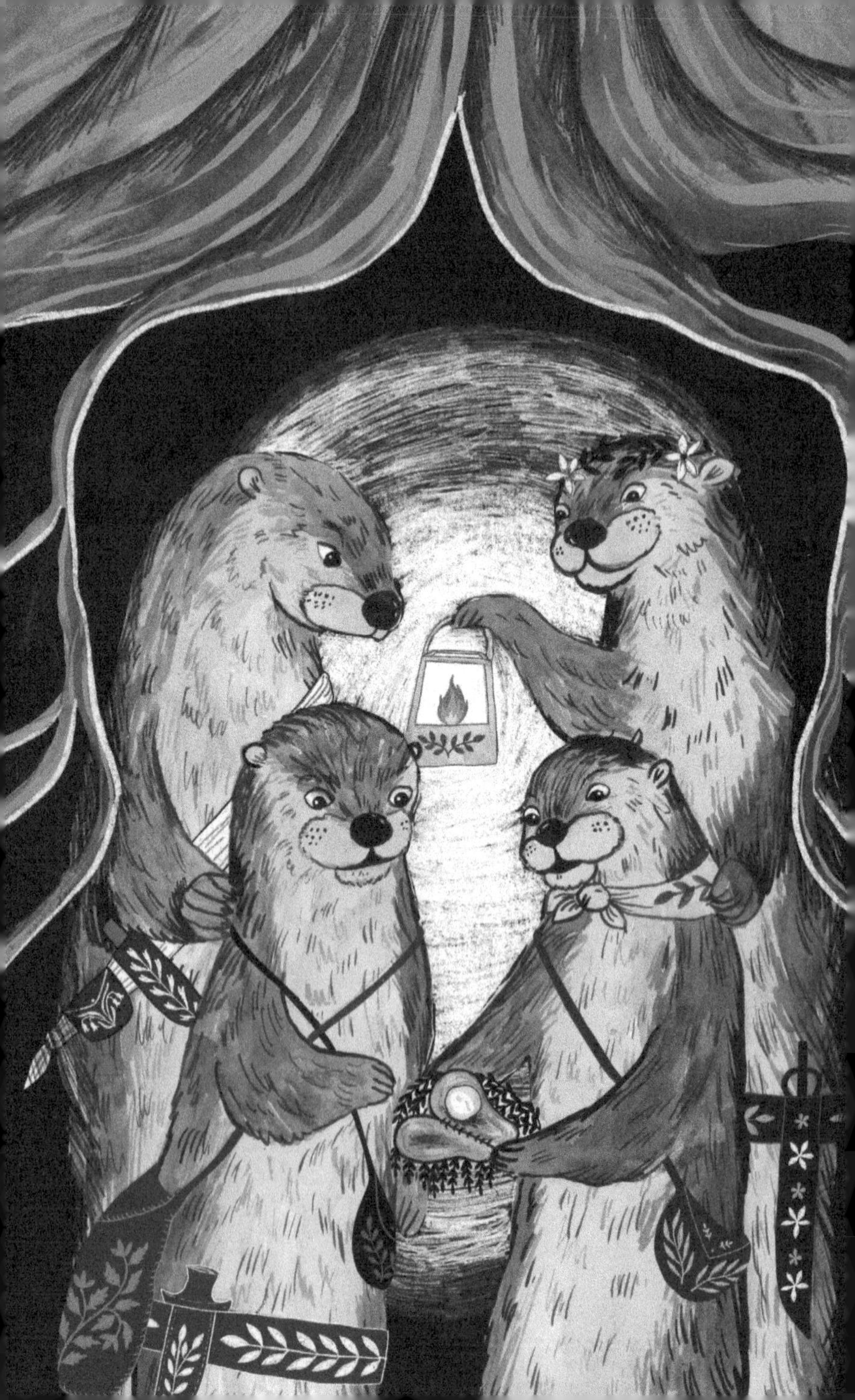

This shell still had both parts hinged together, and it had been fashioned into a box, the hinge carefully bound with thread to keep it strong. Both sides were finely pierced and engraved with swirling patterns, like the ripples on the river.

'Look inside,' he told Silken, and she lifted the top shell and gasped. The mother of pearl lining of the shell had been polished to a gleaming shine, but it was the pearl in the centre that drew all their eyes. It was as long as one of Sedge's own claws, and it shone with a soft light. Silken closed the shell even more carefully than she'd opened it, and wrapped it back up.

'What if I lose it?' she muttered to Sedge.

'We won't. Here, strap it round.' He helped her tie the parcel across her front, and slung the satchel of food around his own shoulders.

'There's a letter in there too,' Lady Thorn explained. 'I've suggested to Master Grey that we meet at Oak Island, at the new moon.' Sedge saw that she was twisting her paws together, the same way he did when he was troubled. 'Do you remember it from your journey? Three days from here, a little island in the middle of the stream, with two great oak trees. Better for us to meet and talk on neutral territory, I think.' She sighed. 'That's assuming they come at all, of course.'

'They'll be there,' said Silken.

'We'll make them come with us, Ma,' added Sedge. 'I promise. We'll see you soon.'

And with a final nuzzle of whiskers from their mother, the brother and sister slipped into the water together, darting down the river and glancing back every so often at their two watchers.

Sedge shook himself in the water, suddenly ashamed at the bubble of glee that was rising up inside him. Away from the holt. Out on their own.

Free.

CHAPTER FIVE

Sedge had fished and gathered along the waters within a day's swim from the holt many times, so for the first part of their journey, he knew the river well. Beyond that were the stretches of the river that he'd only explored once before, while he was searching for Silken – or Elderberry as he'd thought of her then. But as the days passed, days of carefree swimming and singing, he and Silken had gone further than he'd ever been before. Now they were close to the lodge. The river was new, and so different. It was wider and deeper, a broad ribbon of water winding through more open grasslands, with clumps of great trees here and there.

'We'll be there soon,' Silken said quietly. She seemed smaller this morning, Sedge thought, even though he wasn't sure how that could be. She was paddling neatly along the shallower edge of the river, with none of her usual exuberant dives and twirls.

'Are you all right?' he asked.

'Mmm. Nervous, I suppose.' She glanced sideways at him. 'Some of the beavers didn't . . . like me. I was too strange and wrong. Now I'm coming back to them as an otter. I'm proud of that, really I am, and I want to show them my true self. But some will feel like Celandine does – that otters are for otters and beavers are for beavers, and that's the way it should be. What I said about growing up being told that otters want to make beaver kits into fur hats wasn't me trying to be funny.'

Sedge nodded. 'Well. I suppose at least I'll be there. If that's helpful,' he added, suddenly realising how conceited it sounded – as though he could solve everything. 'If they want to say things about otters, they'll have to say it to both of us.'

'It does help.' She nudged against him gratefully, and then peered forward at the turn of the river. 'Only a little further. I expect they've seen us by now – the scouts, I mean. Someone will have headed back to the lodge to tell them we're coming.'

Sedge tried not to look around for the scouts, tried hard to seem unconcerned, but he could feel the fur prickling over the top of his head. Silken's foster-father was the only beaver he had ever seen, and now he was about to meet a full lodge, some of them probably hostile.

'There it is.' Silken led him down a wide backwater, and Sedge stopped, frozen in the water, staring at the dam.

Silken had tried to explain to him what the dam was like,

but he'd had no idea how huge it was. It stretched across the width of the channel, a great pile of wood – and not only sticks, but branches, tree trunks too. The dam blocked the whole channel, holding back the flow of the river. The water built up before it in a great, deep pool, and at last Sedge understood Silken's pride in her foster-father's building.

'They made this?' he whispered to her, stopping at the edge of the pool, and gazing around at the quiet loveliness.

'Yes.' Silken turned slowly in the water, admiring the pool, and the dam, and domed lodge beside it. 'It's strange, coming back to see it again as a – as someone who doesn't belong,' she finished, rather wistfully.

'It's so different from the holt. I didn't understand when you were telling me about it before. It's so clever.' Sedge shivered, and Silken looked round at him in surprise.

'What's wrong?'

'It seems almost *too* clever,' he murmured. 'To shape the river for one's own purposes. Imprisoning her waters in a pool like this, just so that your doorway is always under the surface. It frightens me.'

Silken cast him one troubled glance, but that was all she could do, for just then a thickly furred head popped up in front of them, and then another and another, until they were surrounded by staring beavers.

Sedge drew a little closer to his sister, unsure whether he was protecting her, or asking her to protect him. He tried not to stare back too boldly at the crowd surrounding them, but he didn't want to look as though he was frightened either. He gazed mildly around the circle, nodding politely when the beavers met his eyes.

'Silken. Daughter . . .' The largest of the beavers swam forward, gently placing one heavy paw against Silken's muzzle. 'I hadn't meant to call you that,' he added slowly. 'I know you've found your true family now. But I couldn't help it.'

'You were my father all that time,' Silken said, her voice shaking. 'You were very generous to take me in. I understand that now. Not many would have done, especially just after a flood.'

A few of the beavers in the circle around them nodded or grunted at this, as though they agreed. Sedge wasn't sure they had approved of Master Grey's decision. Silken had been right, he thought. Not all of the lodge welcomed their return. He moved closer to his sister again, his fur brushing against hers. He was *definitely* protecting her, even if she didn't need it.

'And this is your brother? I saw him, when I followed you along the river . . .' The old beaver lowered his voice, as though he was rather ashamed to have chased after them so secretively.

The quiet sadness in his words struck Sedge, and he bowed his head gracefully to Silken's protector. 'I must thank you, Master Grey,' he said. 'My mother asked me to make sure and pass along her messages – and we've brought a gift and another letter from her – but I want to thank you myself. All this time I'd forgotten I even had a sister. The otters at Greenriver thought that perhaps the flood had damaged my memories, or that my fear of the rising water had made me forget. Once I remembered, I knew I had to find my sister again. But I didn't wish to drag her away from you, the way the river took her from me.'

The grizzled beaver looked at Sedge properly for the first time, his dark eyes surprised and grateful. 'You are a kind creature,' he murmured, and then he spoke up louder. 'All of you beavers – we must bring Silken and her brother into the lodge and welcome them properly.'

A worried whispering hiss ran around the circle of beavers at this, but no one spoke up against him. He dived under the surface, followed by the pair of otters.

Sedge was curious to see inside the lodge – the great domed mass of sticks looked impressive from the outside, even if it was quite messy. They emerged into a short tunnel, all of them briskly shaking the water out of their fur, and the Master Builder led them into a large open room, a great hall much like the one back at Greenriver Holt. But as Sedge looked around admiringly, he saw that the walls were decorated with patterns and pictures in different colours of clay, something he had never seen before.

'Your walls!' he exclaimed delightedly, turning to see all around. 'Silken, you didn't tell me about this!'

Silken blinked at him in surprise. 'I didn't think of it. I suppose they are beautiful, especially if you've not seen such things before.'

'I can see all the different plants,' Sedge told her, pacing eagerly around, and forgetting the beavers staring at him. 'Birds too! These are incredible. We have nothing like this at the holt, Master Grey. Oh! Silken, our present.' He hurried back, looking guilty, but Silken's foster-father nodded at him, his eyes crinkling at the corners, as if he were pleased.

'I take a great deal of pleasure in our wall paintings too. It's good to see that beavers and otters admire the same beautiful things.'

Sedge nodded a little doubtfully, remembering that the beavers had not appreciated Silken's singing at all. Now wasn't the moment to say so, though. Instead he helped Silken to untie the pouch slung around her shoulders, so she could present their mother's gift.

Master Grey cupped the carved river mussel shell in his

paws delightedly, holding the pearl out to the other beavers to admire.

'I have never seen one so fine,' he declared. 'We shall set it in a place of honour, for all of us to admire.'

'Pretty gifts to make us forget our duty as a lodge,' someone muttered, just loud enough for Sedge to hear. He managed not to swing round and glare at the speaker, just. Most of the beavers seemed to be genuinely pleased by his mother's gift, murmuring appreciatively as they came up to stroke the glowing pearl and exclaim over the delicate carving of the shell.

'There's a letter from our mother, as well,' Silken murmured to Master Grey. 'It's – it's important. There's news from further up the river . . . But we should let her tell it. You should read it . . . away from here.'

Master Grey nodded slowly, a frown creasing his muzzle.

'Silken!' A large beaver appeared next to them and picked up his sister, grabbing her so tightly that she squeaked. Sedge tensed and stepped forward, ready to intervene – although the young beaver was so enormous that he wasn't sure what he'd be able to do.

'Put me down, you great lump!' Silken said, but she didn't sound angry at all. 'Oh, Frost, I've missed you! Where's Speckle?' she added, as Frost set her on her paws again.

Sedge watched as a smaller beaver with a pattern of light spots across her muzzle flung herself at Silken, patting her shoulders and muzzle and ears as though checking that she was all in one piece. 'How could you just up and leave?' she demanded. 'We thought you'd been eaten!' Here she cast a worried, rather embarrassed look at Sedge. 'I didn't mean that *you* would have eaten her,' she said quickly, but she didn't sound all that sure.

'Speckle, Frost, this is Sedge. He's my brother,' Silken said. She'd gone shy, Sedge realised, her eyes on the ground as if she wasn't sure how her friends would react to him. At least the rest of the crowd was still admiring the pearl, which gave them a chance to talk a little more privately. It wouldn't be too obvious if Silken's friends were to snub him. Sedge straightened his spine, eyeing the two beavers uncertainly.

Frost nodded, giving him the same look back, and then seemed to cast caution to the wind. He clapped Sedge on the back with a mighty paw, and Sedge just about managed not to fall over. 'Welcome, friend!'

'Er, thank you,' Sedge murmured breathlessly, trying to ignore Silken, who was now smirking at him.

'Silken, we were so shocked when the Master Builder came back and told us where you had gone!' Speckle said. 'I never thought that you were . . .' She looked at Sedge and shrugged apologetically. 'An *otter.*' She didn't say *one of those creatures*, but Sedge could hear it in her tone.

'I am,' Silken told her stoutly. 'And I'm proud of it, and proud of my brother.'

'Well said.' Frost gave a solemn nod. 'It does make a lot of sense, come to think of it. You were never . . .'

'Much use as a beaver?' Silken suggested helpfully.

'Here now, I didn't say that!' Frost gazed at her, aghast.

Silken snorted, and nudged her brother. 'He's a lot of fun to tease, this one,' she pointed out.

'We should get on then,' Sedge told Frost. 'She spends most of her time teasing me, these days.'

'She's too clever by half,' Frost growled, but he didn't really sound cross. 'I can't believe you two went that far up the river – and then came straight back down again! And what's all this about two otters killing the night wolf? Is the story true? Was that you two?'

Sedge shrugged and nodded. He didn't want to tell the whole thing again, but luckily Frost and Speckle seemed to see that in his expression. Frost merely thumped him on the back again, and Speckle whispered, 'Thank you.'

Sedge heard it then, in the embarrassed silence. Just the faintest whisper, travelling among the watching beavers.

'Look at them. Dirty murdering beasts.'

Silken had warned him, but he still froze in shock. Master Grey had been so welcoming, and Frost and Speckle were clearly delighted to see Silken, even if they were a little nervous of him.

'*Poor Master Grey,*' the hissing whisper continued. '*Duped again. How long did we harbour that evil creature? It's a wonder we weren't all murdered in our beds.*'

'*She nearly killed little Brindle,*' another whisper came back.

'*Oh, I haven't forgotten . . .*'

Sedge shivered at the viciousness in that whisper. Who was it speaking? He tried to peer sideways, without making it too obvious what he was doing, but there were still a large crowd of beavers massed together, all chattering and murmuring, and it was impossible to pick out the whisperers. Most of the crowd kept turning to look at him and Silken, and he couldn't read their expressions – their features were unfamiliar, and they were half hidden behind their longer fur.

'Did you hear that?' he asked Silken quietly. 'Someone isn't pleased to see you.' Then he felt guilty as he saw her flinch.

'No. But I told you not everyone would be welcoming.'

Frost and Speckle glanced round uneasily, and Sedge gave them a narrow-eyed look. 'They said something about Silken nearly killing someone called Brindle.'

'Not that again,' Frost growled.

'But at least it tells us who it was,' Speckle put in, sighing. 'Tawny – which isn't much of a surprise.'

'I didn't nearly kill anyone,' Silken said quickly to Sedge. 'It was an accident, when we were rebuilding. Brindle's one of the littlest kits. He wasn't even hurt. But his mother – that's Tawny – she blamed me.'

Sedge was silent for a moment, gazing at her. 'But you still half believe it *was* your fault, don't you?'

Silken shrugged, and Sedge longed to hug her as Frost had – but he didn't want her to pull away, embarrassed in front of her old friends. 'Back then everything seemed to be my fault,' she murmured.

Sedge let out a stifled, exasperated snarl. 'It was all very well for your foster-father to take you in, but he should have tried to find who you really belonged to. It was all wrong for you, growing up here.'

'Now, wait a minute—' Frost started to say, but then a heavy paw landed on his shoulder.

'The otter is right,' Master Grey said slowly, even as Sedge looked round for someone to hide behind, and Silken hung her head. 'I should have tried harder. And we should have talked, Silken. Perhaps—' He looked at her shyly for a moment. 'Perhaps you and your brother would talk with me now? Shall we walk out along the dam, as we used to?'

Silken nodded eagerly, and Sedge scurried after them, still cursing his loose tongue as Master Grey led the way back down the entrance tunnel. The three of them popped up into the deep pool, surfacing just below the dam. Silken and her foster-father scrambled out on to a worn and flattened log that was obviously the usual landing spot, and Master Grey climbed slowly up the side of the dam. Sedge followed him and Silken up on to the pathway along the top of the strange construction, looking around curiously. His wonder at the building was edging away a little of his embarrassment – but it was still there. As Master Grey gazed out at the river backing up behind his dam, Sedge took a deep breath and burst out, 'I shouldn't have said that, about this place being all wrong for Silken. I'm sorry. I'm supposed to be here to help us work together—'

Master Grey gave a little chuckling snort, and Sedge eyed him doubtfully. He didn't sound angry. He sounded a bit like Teasel, in fact. On one of her good days.

'Honest words, those were. Sticking up for my little Silken. I like to hear it.' He sighed. 'And you were right.' He turned to Silken and inclined his head – almost in a bow. 'I apologise.'

Silken blinked at him. 'What for?'

'My selfishness. When the swan first brought you here in the aftermath of the flood, all was confusion. The water surge had broken through the dam, and then lapped up into the hall of the lodge, weakening the clay binding. We were so frantic we didn't know if we were coming or going. And then there you were. I had no time to work out what to do with you – so I kept you. Never meaning it to be for ever, of course not. I knew that you weren't really ours. But by the time we had everything straight again, you'd started following me around. You chattered.'

He stopped, and Sedge saw that he was fighting with his words. 'I'd missed having someone to talk to,' he went on at last. 'My mate had died, you see. At the darkest part of the winter, when the pool was icing over at the edges . . . She'd been sickening for a long while, and she slipped away. My Silky.'

Silken was staring at him, struck silent, and Sedge frowned at her. 'You named Silken after her?' he asked.

Master Grey shrugged helplessly. 'And for her coat. Softer than a beaver's pelt. It came to mind . . .'

'I never knew that. You never spoke of her,' Silken whispered. 'All I knew about her was that you treasured her green scarf.'

'It's what I regret most,' her foster-father said slowly. 'Letting you think that she was your mother.' He nodded to Sedge. 'Your brother is right. I should have tried to find your people. Especially as you grew, and it became clearer and clearer that you weren't just a strange little beaver kit. But I couldn't bear to. I was selfish, as I say.'

Silken laid a paw on his, and Sedge saw how narrow it was against the beaver's heavy claws. 'I'm grateful. You could just have cast me out. I'd never have survived, all on my own.'

Master Grey patted her gently. 'But then you had to set out alone anyway. I should have told you all of this, before you became so desperate. I knew it – I was working up to it, but I hadn't the courage. It makes me glad now, to see you with your own family.' He nodded to Sedge. 'Loved and protected, and protecting him in turn.'

'I miss you, still,' Silken whispered, and the old beaver pulled her close, holding her tight.

The look between them made Sedge turn away. He gazed sternly at the shallow waters beyond the dam.

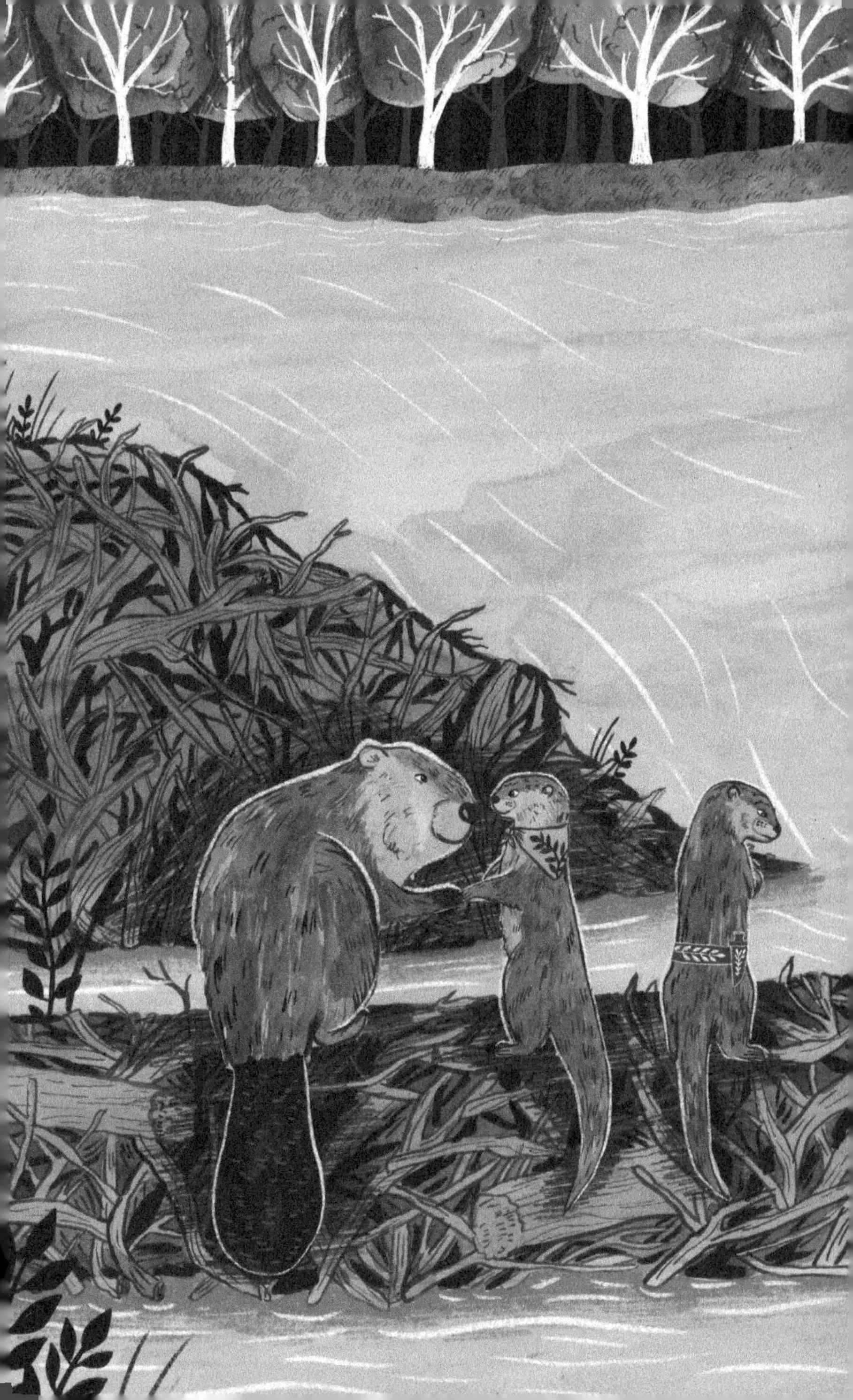

CHAPTER SIX

Silken. Silken.

She woke abruptly, unsure how long she had been sleeping. Someone was calling her. She sat up on the reed bed, blinking as her eyes adjusted to the blackness of the chamber. Sedge was still fast asleep, twitching and snuffling in the reeds, and she couldn't hear her foster-father at all. Neither of them had woken her.

There was silence now. Maybe she had dreamed the voice.

Sedge and Silken were sharing Silken's old room at the lodge, a small one linked to Master Grey's chamber. It was right at the end of a passageway. They had fallen asleep right away, worn out by their journey and the strange, tense atmosphere that had persisted all through dinner in the main hall. Master Grey had read their mother's letter to the lodge after their walk along the dam, and the news about the foxes had been a terrible shock. It did mean there was something for the beavers to worry and gossip about apart from her strange return, but Lady Thorn's plea for help hadn't gone down very well. The unpleasant whispers and sidelong looks had grown more and more obvious as the meal drew on. The otter cubs had picked politely at the dishes, and Silken wondered how she had managed for so long without the fish her otter body needed. After the meal they'd sneaked out to fish for their supper, under cover of an evening swim.

Now, as Silken rubbed her paws over her muzzle, she heard a scuffle of paws outside in the passageway. Paws and whispers. It was the dark of the night – no one should be wandering around the lodge, surely? The scuffling stopped, and Silken counted breaths. Her own. Sedge's snuffling. And . . . someone else waiting outside the opening to the chamber, their breathing fast and anxious.

Silken leaned over, setting her muzzle close to Sedge's ear. 'Wake up,' she murmured. 'Sedge, wake up quick. I'm worried.'

She caught the dark shine of her brother's eyes and he wriggled upright. 'What is it?' Then he whipped round to look at the doorway, hearing the patter of steps. He was up in a moment, reaching for the little stone knife he always carried. He hadn't taken it off when they had settled down to sleep.

'It's us,' someone hissed from the doorway. 'Stop waving that at me.'

'Frost? What are you doing?' Silken demanded. 'It's the middle of the night.'

'We need to wake Master Grey.' Speckle pushed her way round Frost and into the bedchamber. 'There's something going on. Tawny and her cronies are making trouble. They're having some sort of meeting in the main hall.'

'I heard them on the way back from the kitchens,' Frost explained. He looked mildly embarrassed. 'I was hungry . . . It was a long time since dinner. I poked my head round the door and saw them. They're all in there, riling one another up. They were talking about . . . about exiling Master Grey.'

Silken gasped. She knew Tawny hated her, but she'd never expected that anger to go any further than evil gossip.

'They've been complaining and spreading rumours for ages, but it's as if you and Sedge being here's sent them wild.' Speckle shot an anxious glance back at the passageway. 'The news you brought, about the foxes . . .'

'At dinner last night I heard some of Tawny's gang saying that Master Grey betrayed the lodge by taking you in,' Frost told them, frowning. 'That he abandoned us all when he went chasing after you up the river, and now he's brought you back and he's going to let otters take over the lodge. They think you're going to force us all up the river to fight the foxes for you.'

'What?' Sedge shook his head. 'That's nonsense. We were asking for help, that's all!'

'We know it's not true,' Speckle agreed, sighing. 'But it's the kind of nonsense that makes beavers scared. Scared means you believe. Tawny wants everyone scared so they'll listen to her silliness.'

Silken shivered, remembering the hate in Tawny's eyes, back when Brindle had almost been hurt by the falling tree trunk. Tawny wanted to hurt her in return, Silken was sure of it.

'But surely no one's going to listen to her.' Sedge looked at the others. 'Everyone will see that it's all made up. Won't they? Master Grey isn't in thrall to otters. He wrote a letter to our mother saying how much he missed Silken, that was all. He hasn't even said he wants to help us against the foxes yet. He said it would need to be discussed with the elders of the lodge.'

'Even *considering* it is too much for some of our lodge,' Frost said bitterly. 'But there's no time for talking about it now – we need to wake Master Grey, let him know what's happening. He can rouse the rest of the lodge, the beavers who are loyal to him.'

'Then what happens?' Silken whispered worriedly. 'A fight?'

'I hope not . . .' Frost said. 'But maybe.'

Silken padded over to her father's chamber, peering in. 'He's not here!' she burst out, swinging round anxiously. 'Do you think they've taken him? Oh – no, I bet I know where he is.' She sighed. 'Out on the dam. Whenever he can't sleep, or he's worried, that's where he goes.'

But Sedge looked even more fearful. 'If it's known that he goes out there often at night, maybe they waited for him to leave. The entrance tunnel would be easy enough to barricade. With him outside, they can take control of your lodge without him being here to fight back.'

Frost stamped one paw. 'They can't!'

'I'm not letting them do this,' Silken hissed. 'My foster-father spent his whole life working for the lodge. Tawny isn't going to steal it from him just because he was kind-hearted enough to take me in after the flood. We have to warn him! He needs to be here – half Tawny's support will melt away once they see he's no traitor.'

'Can we get out and find him, without them seeing us?' Sedge asked.

'It'd be tricky. The entrance leads off the main chamber, and that's where they were gathering,' Speckle whispered. 'All the passages lead back to it. We could try and creep through . . .'

'Then let's do that. Because sooner or later they're going to send someone to find me and Silken, aren't they?'

Silken swallowed. She had put them all at risk by coming back, she saw it now. She had been so eager to carry back the news of the foxes, and it hadn't been just to warn the lodge. She had wanted to show them all how well she was doing. Her father, Speckle and Frost – even Tawny and her foul gang of gossips. She'd wanted to show off, and now her friends were going to pay for it.

Sedge peered out along the passageway, his whiskers twitching and jittering with nerves. The others were distracted by the fear and horror of being betrayed by the lodge, their family. But the anger inside him was bitter and cold and kept him focused. He was not going to let the lodge hurt Silken again. They would have to go through him first.

No one was in the passage. He glanced back at the others and beckoned, then padded quietly along the dirt floor. As they came close to the end, where the tunnel led into the main chamber, the four of them began to hear voices, and Sedge slowed, flattening himself right against the earth wall. Some of the lamps in the main chamber had been lit, and their soft

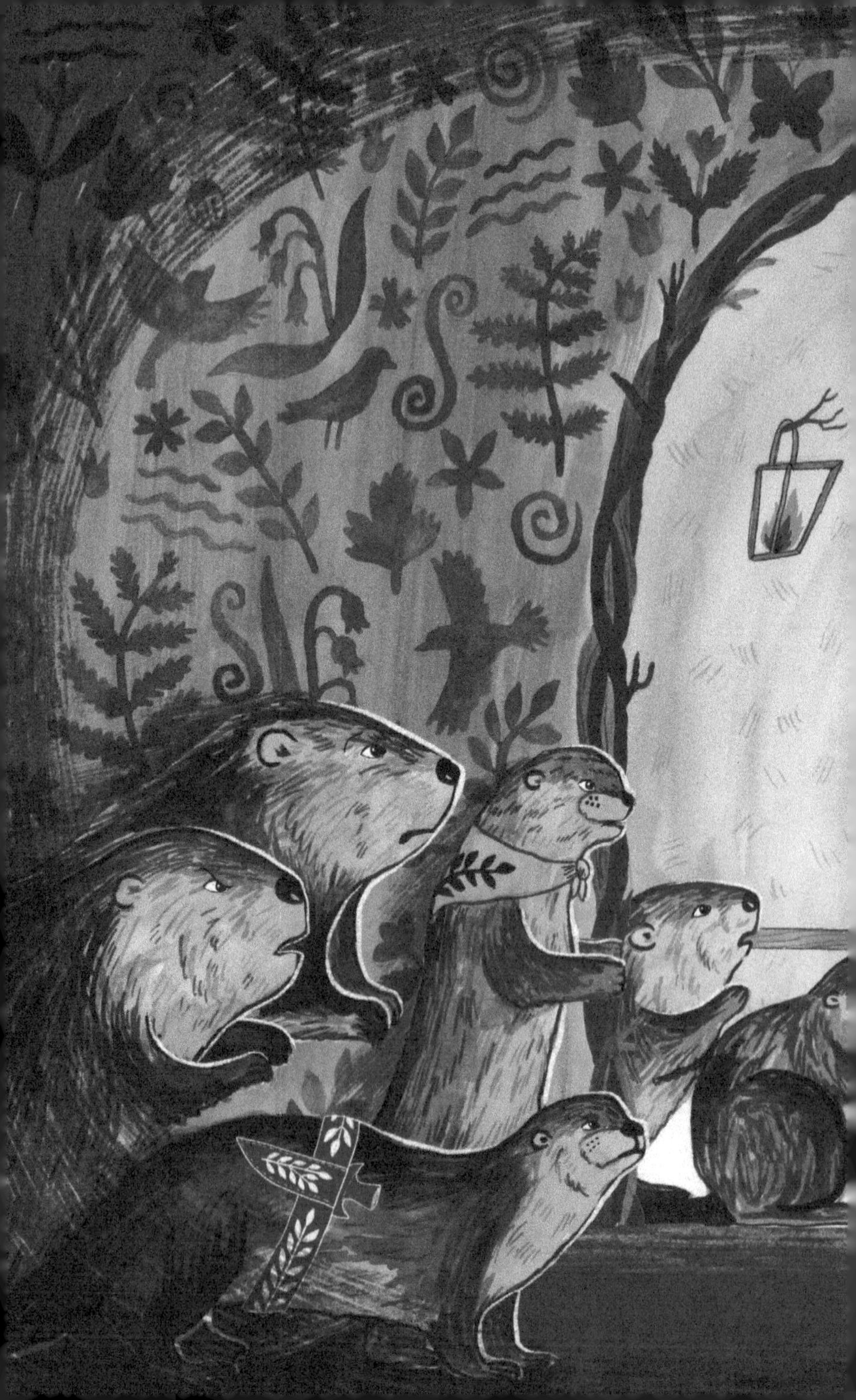

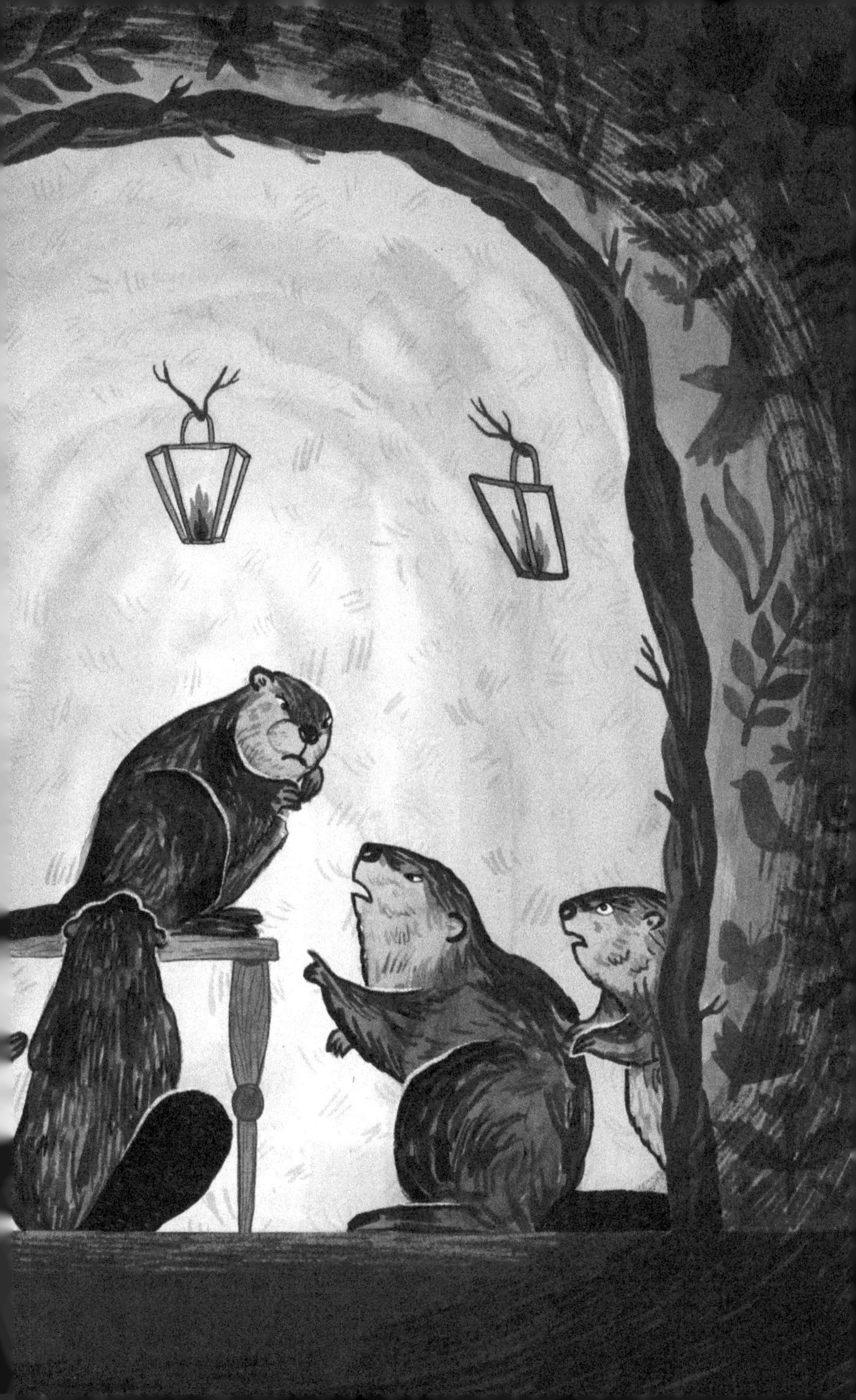

glow reached into the tunnel. He could just see the others pressed nervously behind him.

'That's Tawny,' Silken breathed in his ear, and he nodded. He was almost sure it was the same nasty, bitter voice he had heard whispering earlier on. They listened in silence.

'He's been leading the lodge for too long!' the voice cried. 'He takes us all for granted, you see. He thinks he can do whatever he wants and we'll just say, *Yes, of course, Master Grey. Whatever you want, Master Grey. Let us serve you, Master Grey.*'

'Now then . . .' someone grumbled. 'I don't remember Master Grey treating us like that. Us beavers chose him as our leader.'

'But that was before that creature came along and bewitched him, wasn't it?' Tawny pointed out. Her voice had changed now – she sounded quite reasonable. She was clever, Sedge thought. She could shape her words to fit her listener. 'He was grieving his dear mate, and he had no kits of his own. Just the right moment for her to arrive, wasn't it? Washed up in the flood, or so she'd have us believe . . .'

Sedge caught Silken's sharp intake of breath. Tawny thought she'd only been pretending? Speckle caught Silken's paw, patting at it fiercely.

'Don't you listen . . .' she breathed.

'We need to know what she's saying,' Silken whispered to her. 'To be able to stop her.'

The same beaver who'd grumbled before said, 'What a load of stinking slime. I saw that kit when she first turned up, we all did. She was half drowned and not much bigger than a water rat. She hardly even spoke to start with. It took till midsummer for her to turn into a little chatterbox. She was no spy for the otter holt. You're building a plot out of air and bubbles.'

'He's fighting back for you, whoever he is,' Sedge told them, edging his muzzle round the wall of the passageway. He could see into the main chamber now. Tawny was standing on one of the tables, her paw raised. She was trying to look proud and noble, Sedge thought. There was a crowd of beavers around her – perhaps half the lodge? It was hard to tell, but there definitely weren't as many as earlier in the day, when he and Silken had been welcomed by the Master Builder. The crowd was looking uncertainly between the arguing beaver and Tawny, who was shaking her head and sighing.

'That's my uncle!' Frost muttered, half delighted, half horrified.

'Silvertip?' Speckle whispered, peering over Sedge's shoulder. 'Why's he out here to start with? Who thought *he* was going to join in a plot?'

'Everyone knows he likes a good argument,' Frost said, grinning. 'I suppose they forgot that he's one of Master Grey's strongest workers on the dam.'

'He's practically my father's second in command.' Silken snorted quietly.

'You lot woke me up and dragged me out here saying there was some sort of emergency,' Silvertip growled. 'And now I see what your emergency is. Insurrection and disloyalty. You should be ashamed. Get back to your chambers – and tomorrow if there's some true grievance buried under this pile of dung –' some of the younger beavers at the back of the crowd tittered – 'then we'll bring it to a council of the lodge, instead of this dirty midnight meeting.'

There was a wave of uncomfortable shuffling and muttering among the crowd. The beavers glanced sideways at one another, as if they'd been caught doing something they shouldn't.

'Ah, my friends . . .' Tawny was shaking her head again, eyes wide and whiskers drooping in exaggerated sadness. 'Listen to that. What else should we expect from one of Master Grey's closest cronies, though? I had hoped . . . Well, I suppose it was too much to ask that the rot hadn't spread deeper through our beloved lodge. We must cut it out, before the disease fells the whole tree.'

'I'm a disease, am I?' Silvertip roared. 'Loyal to the Master

Builder, and that makes me rotten now? Are you listening to her? Use your own minds, you feeble lot!'

'Oh . . .' Sedge murmured, ducking back a little. He had a feeling that wasn't going to go down well. Arguments at the holt always got a lot worse when otters started calling each other stupid.

'You see!' Tawny whirled round, stomping to the edge of the table and shaking her paw at him. 'That's what they think of us! This one works right at Master Grey's shoulder! They think we're fools! Mindless, feeble – he said it, not me! They think they can lead us around like kits and we'll do whatever they want. *Do* use your minds – and then your voices! And your paws! Show them we won't be led sleepwalking into slavery! Fight!'

'Fight!' yelled a couple of the excitable younger beavers at the back of the crowd. 'Fight!'

'Fight for your freedom!' Tawny screamed, practically dancing up and down on the table.

'*That's* why she wanted Silvertip,' Silken growled, under the rising roar from the chamber. 'He's never been known for his tact. If anybody could set their backs up, it would be him. What are we going to do?'

'Wake everybody else?' Sedge suggested. 'Master Grey must have allies who aren't here?'

'I suppose so,' Speckle said, a little doubtfully. 'He doesn't really go round trying to make allies. He just builds . . .'

'Which is as it should be,' Frost growled. 'Building's what we *do*. Master Grey hasn't done anything wrong!'

'Except take me in,' Silken murmured sadly, and she shook off their uncomfortable mutters of reply. 'Surely all this noise is going to wake the rest of the lodge?'

'I think Tawny *wants* everyone awake, now that she's stirred this lot up,' Sedge said, watching worriedly as the beavers in the main chamber argued with Silvertip. 'She wants to start a proper fight.' He started as a beaver shoved Silvertip, hard. 'Hey!'

Tawny's mate didn't seem to have done much damage, since Silvertip was built along the same lines as his nephew Frost, but seeing Silvertip rock a little on his heavy paws made the other beavers bolder. The crowd swirled and hissed around him, swiping and growling, and Silvertip was starting to look concerned as well as angry. He lifted his head and roared, 'Wake up! Ho, the lodge! Awake, and fight!'

'We have to help him,' Silken said, darting forward, but Sedge caught at her paw.

'Don't! Look how she's whipped them up, Silken. They'll see you and they'll get even more vicious. You'll probably make things worse for Silvertip.' He wasn't truly thinking about Silvertip at all. Sedge had seen the fiery glow of hate in Tawny's eyes. He couldn't bear for his sister to get any closer to the angry mob.

'I'm going,' Frost snarled, and he launched out into the melee, knocking beavers left and right as he made for his uncle. Speckle chittered worriedly and dashed after him.

A sleepy-looking beaver hurried up the passage behind them. 'What's happening? What's all this noise?'

'It's Tawny,' Silken told her, hesitating a little. 'She's saying that Master Grey is betraying the lodge . . . It's a revolt.'

The beaver suddenly looked a lot more awake. 'Fur and feathers! We're not having that! I'll wake the rest of the builders.' She darted back down the passage, shouting.

'Well, that's good.' Sedge slumped back against the wall, but Silken was still trying to pull her paws out of his grasp.

'We can't just do nothing!'

Sedge tightened his paws on hers. She was right – they couldn't skulk here in a tunnel while her friends were fighting, especially when it was Silken and her father they were fighting for. 'You're right,' he muttered. 'But there's no point trying to join in with that lot, it won't help. We came out here to try and get to your father.' Sedge shrugged. 'He should have the chance to fight for his holt, at least.'

Silken gulped and nodded. 'Let's go. Around the edge of the chamber, in the shadows. Yes?'

'Yes.' He crept after her, and the two of them scurried and dodged along the wall, until they came closer to the knot of tussling beavers. Silken paused, not wanting to be seen, and Sedge tapped her shoulder, pointing at the long table, a few tail-lengths into the main room.

'Underneath!' he whispered, and her eyes glittered in fierce agreement. They shot under the table, racing four-footed as fast as they could under its cover. Thuds and screeches and thumps echoed overhead as more beavers poured into the chamber, and the fight grew darker – and dirtier.

'Maybe we should stop and help them,' Sedge growled, as a stool exploded into splinters a tail-length away.

'No.' Silken edged her muzzle out at the end of the table. 'You were right – we need to get to my father and tell him what's happening. Let's get to that next table. After that we'll be much closer to the entrance tunnel. And I'll bet there won't be any guards in it, for once. Come on.'

They flung themselves across the shadowy gap and under the second table, dodging round the stools and benches until a solid lump of shadow lurking under the table suddenly unfolded into a beaver. Silken was going so fast that she practically barged into them.

'Tawny!' she gasped, reeling back, and for the first time since their fight with the night wolf, Sedge saw her truly afraid.

Tawny shrieked with glee, reaching out to seize Silken, but Sedge was faster. He snapped furiously, his sharp fish-eater's teeth closing on Tawny's thick pelt. The beaver drew back in shock. She looked almost disbelieving – as if she'd never expected someone to actually hurt her.

'Get away from my sister!' Sedge hissed. Then his muzzle wrinkled in a frown. 'And what were you doing skulking under here anyway?'

'She was hiding from the fight!' Silken said, in a high, nervous sort of squeak. 'She's got everyone else fighting for her, why should she dirty her paws?'

'Lies!' Tawny yelped. 'All lies! What else would I expect from you?' She threw herself half out from under the table, slumping to the floor as though grievously injured. 'Help! Help!' she shrieked. 'They've trapped me! Help!'

Sedge and Silken exchanged a panicked glance. Was there time to make for the entrance still? Had the growling, yowling mass of beavers even heard Tawny's scream?

Silken peeked out from under the table. 'They're coming. We'd better get our backs to a wall. They'll find us eventually, and that way we'll have the best chance of fighting them off.' She pressed her paw against Sedge's, just for a moment. 'Thank you,' she murmured – and the two otters raced along the length of the table, shooting out by the painted wall that Sedge had admired so fervently only hours before. Six or seven of the closer beavers were casting about for them in the shadows, while Tawny sobbed and whined, but in the dim light of the hall, no one had spotted them yet . . .

'Silken, wait. It's no good us fighting them—'

'We don't have much choice!'

'But we do! There's one thing you have that Tawny doesn't,' Sedge told his sister urgently. 'She can't sing, Silken. You said the beavers listened to your songs, even if they didn't understand why you sang. Your songs are stronger now, you know they are.' The heavy steps were coming closer as the beavers sniffed them out in the darkness.

'No one's going to hear me over the fighting,' Silken whispered miserably. 'And I don't think they'll want to listen . . .' But she slipped her paws from Sedge's and stepped a little further out from the wall. She closed her eyes and lifted her muzzle, as if she was calling the song to come to her. Sedge moved to her shoulder, ready to push back against any rebel beavers who came close.

Silken began to sing. Her clear voice cut through the shouting and the darkness, and Sedge saw the searching beavers stumble as the jolting rhythm caught them. The song swelled out across the room as a tumbling waterfall of echoes.

All those living by the river
Seek the blessing of the water.
Water brings us all together.
Here I sing the river's message
Made for all of us her children –
Set aside your angry fighting.

The roar of the angry mob stilled to an eerie silence. Sedge thought he could hear the beavers listening. Those who had been searching for them were staring wide-eyed at Silken. There was a need, a longing for the song to go on – Sedge could feel it there in the shadowy chamber.

Tawny was still lying between the tables, but she was curled up into a ball now, and her paws were pressed over her ears, almost as if she was trying to block out the song.

Sedge nodded encouragingly at his sister. She went on.

Listen, I will sing her message,
We all now belong together.
Carried in her rushing currents
Curled and sleeping in her tall reeds.
Fed and rocked and carried onward
We are all her treasured creatures.
Peace we ask of you, our river.

> *Peace, an end to all our warring.*
> *Peace we beg for all your children . . .*

There was an aching, waiting silence as the song ended.

'Look!' Silken whispered shakily, nudging him with one paw and pointing across the room. She seemed dazed – she was still in the strange half-dream of her song, Sedge realised. He wasn't sure what she was pointing at, or why the beavers gathering at the entrance to the lodge looked so worried. Then he realised that the dark shadow staining the floor of the chamber was water. The river had crept in while Silken was singing, seeping up the entranceway and inside the warm, dry lodge. The water drained away as he watched, leaving only a faint, damp gleam behind.

'You called her?' he whispered to Silken, and as she nodded, her eyes caught the light of a hanging lantern and they flashed a strange, silvery glow. Sedge wondered what she had seen in the water – whether there had been a pale otter watching them.

A voice broke through the thick quiet, a polite, gentle voice that meant to be answered. 'All awake, my friends?'

Master Grey walked in through the entrance tunnel, the last thin skin of water parting and slipping away under his paws. Sedge had thought him bunchy and clumsy before – all beavers looked that way to a skinny otter – but now his heavy figure seemed dignified.

The beavers shuffled and whispered and looked away, but Silvertip and Frost came striding forward.

'Are you all right?' Silvertip demanded, in a low rumble. 'They didn't hurt you? I thought perhaps she'd sent some of those fools out to the dam to attack.'

'Tawny?' Master Grey sighed. 'I never thought she'd go that far.' He looked around worriedly, and called, 'Silken? Where is she? And her brother?'

'We're here.' Silken shook off the last traces of her song and hurried to meet him. 'Tawny's over there,' she added, pointing. Tawny was curled up on the floor between the tables, mewling. 'I'm not sure what happened to her . . .'

'Whatever it was that came out of your song happened to her,' Frost said bluntly. 'It – *she* – looked at her and Tawny fell apart.'

'You saw Lady River?' Sedge asked curiously. He hadn't expected that, but the beavers were nodding and whispering to one another, looking uncertainly at the dark water stains, all that was left. They had seen *something*. And he hadn't. *I didn't need to see her*, Sedge told himself, trying not to feel jealous.

'That's what you call her then?' Frost let out a whistling

breath. 'Does she – belong only to the otters?' He glanced wistfully at the water-dark earth around the entrance to the lodge.

'I don't think she belongs to anyone,' Sedge said firmly. He was trying to convince himself as much as Frost and the others. 'Otters sing to her. We've done it always, but none of us had seen her, not for so many summers. Only once in our mother's time, I think. She likes Silken's singing – she listens, sometimes. It was her song that rolled back the flood and saved our holt.'

'She walked out by me,' Master Grey said slowly. 'As I came up into the tunnel. She nodded to me.'

'They've called up a monster,' Tawny whispered, and the circle parted to show her standing there, shrunken and trembling.

'How can you say that?' Frost demanded. 'Didn't you see? That was no monster – she was – she was . . .' He trailed off, unsure.

'No one really knows what she is,' Sedge told him. 'But we think of her as the spirit of the river.'

'They've deceived you.' Tawny looked pleadingly around at the other beavers, and Sedge realised that this time, she actually believed what she was saying. Her fear had been a performance before, practised and slick, and it had worked.

Now that she was truly frightened, no one believed her. 'This is all some shameful otter plot. They brought that monster here to hurt us . . .'

Silken stepped forward. 'You're the deceitful one. You were hiding, weren't you?' She nodded at the other beavers, all eyeing Tawny. 'Did you see? She was skulking under the table while you were fighting for her.'

The suspicious, angry whispers grew louder, and Tawny's eyes widened in panic. 'No! Don't listen to her. They sang some sort of binding, didn't you hear it?' She padded around the circle, holding out her paws pleadingly to the beavers who had been her allies before – but they turned away from her.

'Tawny, you should go back to your chamber,' Master Grey said.

'So now you'll shut me up, will you?'

The old builder shook his head wearily. 'No. I won't do anything. That's not how things are in this lodge. If others want to listen to you – well then, they'll listen. But you should rest. You look unwell.'

She glared at him, and they could see her wanting to hiss her defiance. She scuttled away.

'You're really going to leave her to keep dripping her poison?' Silvertip growled. 'So she can sweet-talk these foolish—'

'Master Grey!' Speckle yelped, before Silvertip could destroy all their good work by saying any more. Then she looked horrified when everyone turned to stare at her. 'Um . . . what I wanted to say was – was that Tawny was against us meeting with the otters. She didn't want us to go to Oak Island. And now that she's proved herself a traitor . . .'

'It's a sign.' Frost nodded eagerly. 'We must go to the island and meet with the otters. We *have* to be there.'

Sedge coughed politely and raised his voice. 'Lady Thorn, our mother, is very eager for the meeting to go ahead,' he told the beavers. 'You would honour us with your presence.' He bowed his head.

'The meeting will take place.' Master Grey spoke low in his chest, with just a hint of a growl. 'There will be none of this gossip about plots and monsters. The creatures of the river will stand together. I am still the Master Builder. Unless any here wish to challenge me?'

There was an embarrassed silence, with a great many beavers staring at the earthen floor. At last, Master Grey nodded. 'I will attend, and I will ask several of the elder beavers to come with me. Silvertip, you will remain here to lead the lodge while I am gone.' He looked thoughtfully at Frost and Speckle, now standing protectively close to Silken and Sedge, and added, 'And you two should come with us as well. You can represent the younger beavers at this island meeting.'

Frost roared, 'Yes!' and pounded Sedge on the shoulder with a huge paw. Then he realised what he'd done, and made a fast grab before Sedge toppled over. 'Sorry! Sorry!'

'You're that excited to leave the Stronghold?' Master Grey asked, looking bemused, and Frost sagged a little.

'Well . . . Silken went adventuring up the river. And he –' Frost waved a paw at Sedge, and his voice took on a disbelieving note – 'he fought the night wolf! Killed her! I wouldn't mind seeing what's round a few more bends in the river . . .'

'It wasn't a fight,' Sedge said quietly. 'I crept up behind her and hit her with a rock. When she thought I was already dead. That's not a fight.'

No one spoke for a moment. Then his sister patted gently at his muzzle. 'It may not have been a fight. But it was a rescue. You saved me,' Silken told him. 'You were valiant. And you're going to have to get used to it.'

Master Grey nodded approvingly. 'Indeed. And one more beaver will come with us to the island.' He looked around, gathering all their attention. 'Tawny.'

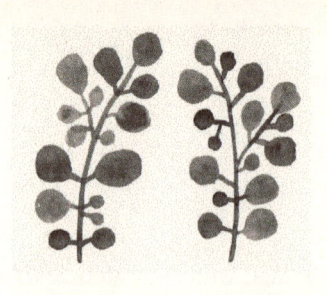

CHAPTER SEVEN

Master Grey's announcement caused consternation among the beavers. Several of his loyal elders wanted Tawny shut up somewhere dark (and then forgotten, preferably) but the Master Builder insisted that it was his duty to keep her close – that he couldn't leave a dangerous creature inside the Stronghold while he was away. So when they set out for the island, which was two days' journey away up the river, Tawny, her mate, Russet, and their little kit, Brindle, swam with them.

They weren't under guard, not exactly. But it was very noticeable that one of the elder beavers was always close by Tawny. She ignored them all, swimming on with Brindle close beside her, or sometimes on her back. Silken stayed out of their way – Tawny obviously hated her, and Silken was fairly sure that she'd have convinced Brindle to hate her too. Even though she kept her distance, Silken could still feel them watching her.

Late in the evening of the second day they approached

the little wooded island where the meeting was to be held. It had been a hard two days' journeying. Master Grey wanted to arrive at the island before the otters from Greenriver, if they could. The otters might have suggested this meeting, but her foster-father didn't want them feeling as if they were in charge.

Sedge and Silken had passed the island on their journey down the river – they had even stopped to rest there. But it looked different now, in the gathering shadows of a summer evening. The trees were still and silent, not a breath of wind stirring their leaves. The whole place seemed to be waiting, and the beavers hushed too, scrambling out of the river and looking around in awe. Even Frost was quiet for once.

'I thought it was smaller than this,' Silken said, looking doubtfully round at the trees. These were the same oaks they'd sheltered under, only a few days before, but they seemed taller now, their trunks heavy and dark.

Sedge nodded. 'It's as if they were expecting us,' he said.

Silken blinked and shook herself as the beavers bustled about gathering sticks and brushwood to build shelters. She was about to dash after Frost and Speckle when Sedge reached out to stop her. Tawny was right behind them. The beaver hissed quietly as she passed, and Silken shivered.

'I feel sorry for him, you know.'

'Who?' Silken glanced round at Sedge's words and spotted

Tawny's kit trundling slowly after her. 'Brindle?' She snorted. She couldn't think of Brindle as anything but Tawny's kit, the little troublemaker who'd panicked and run the wrong way under a falling tree trunk. That had been the beginning of Tawny's revolt.

'He's only little, for a journey like this,' Sedge pointed out.

Master Grey had set a fast pace, fast even for Sedge and Silken, and Brindle was so much younger and smaller. Tawny had carried the kit on her back for a few short spells on the first day, but after that Brindle had swum determinedly by himself, even when Tawny tried to coax him to rest and be carried.

Silken sniffed, which might have been agreement and might not.

'It isn't his fault that Tawny's who she is.'

'Maybe,' Silken said. She looked sideways at Sedge. She knew he'd found it hard being their mother's cub, sometimes. It was a lot to live up to. Perhaps it made him more sympathetic.

Perhaps he was right. Brindle was trailing after Tawny, dragging a bundle of bracken and sticks for the shelter that the beavers had started to make. He seemed very small as he staggered about, and his whiskers were drooping with weariness. He added his sticks to the pile, and as he plodded away to fetch more, he obviously felt Sedge and Silken staring at him. He glanced across, and a little flash of something – hope, maybe – appeared in his eyes, before he turned hurriedly away.

'What was that?' Silken demanded. 'What did he look at us like that for?' She huffed out a breath. 'I can't be thinking about him, I've enough else to worry about.'

'Too late now,' Sedge told her, shrugging. 'You know that's a sign of a born lady of the holt, don't you? You just have to fuss and bother about everyone.'

'Shut up.'

'Yes, my lady.'

Silken showed him her teeth, but Sedge just went on smirking.

'Stop wittering on, you.' Silken growled. 'We'd better help build that shelter. We don't want them thinking that otters are lazy.' She stomped irritably over to Master Grey to ask for instructions, hoping that her foster-father wasn't planning to build anything too complicated. She and Sedge could help gather materials – some of them, at least – but she didn't want to remind the beavers of her silly otter paws and feeble bite, not now.

Then again, with the great meeting about to start, was it better they thought of her as useless, rather than one of those fierce, sharp-clawed otters? She shook the thought away, busying herself with gathering an armful of fallen sticks. The island hardly seemed to be inhabited at all – there were a few quiet bird calls, but otherwise the place seemed eerily empty.

The beavers piled up twigs, reeds and bracken around the largest tree trunks, turning them into tiny rooms. They weren't building only for themselves, Silken realised. There would be enough of the little shelters to house the otters too. Master Grey was taking his duties as a host very seriously. Or, he wanted Lady Thorn and her otters to arrive and find that the beavers had organised everything, and were in charge . . . That was clever. Silken hadn't expected the grizzled old beaver to be quite so sly. She was impressed.

'How will you choose who sleeps where?' she asked him abruptly, as they dropped more bundles of soft reeds at his feet. Sedge glanced at her in surprise, but Master Grey combed his paw through his stubby whiskers and eyed her thoughtfully.

'Well now. That wouldn't be up to me . . .' he murmured, his voice slow and gentle.

Silken put her head on one side. 'Isn't that why you built the shelters? So you could be the one telling our mother what to do and where to go?'

Master Grey sighed, and looked around at the grove of trees and the patch of mossy grass in the middle of the tiny island, and shrugged. 'Beavers one side, otters the other. As always, I suppose . . .'

Silken felt suddenly ashamed of herself. He didn't sound as though he was scheming. Had he just wanted to be welcoming after all?

Master Grey gave her a thoughtful look, and then closed one eyelid in a slow wink. 'Your brother is right, you know,' he told her. 'You notice things, Silken. You always did. And then you worry, and you care, and you try to make things the way they should be. Just like a lady of the holt should, it sounds to me.'

'Were you listening to us?' Sedge stared at him.

'Beavers are known for their very good hearing,' Master Grey said, his dark eyes so solemn that Silken couldn't tell if he were teasing Sedge or not. Somehow, while she was living at the Stronghold, she had never noticed her slow, serious foster-father's sense of humour. 'You notice more of what's going on than you used to, Silken. Since you left us. Perhaps you've been watching your mother. Or the time away from us has simply sharpened your eyes.' He sighed. 'And you're not wrong to say I was trying to gain the upper hand. You four and Silvertip may have put down that uprising back at the Lodge, but Tawny and her friends aren't the only ones who think this is a bad idea. As far as I know, you and your brother are the only otters that the rest of our lodge have ever seen.

Even the elders are terrified, though they're hiding it well. I'll take any advantage I can. Any way to make us feel stronger when the otters climb out of the river.'

Silken lifted her paws in a miserable shrug. 'So . . . the otters haven't even arrived, and already you're trying to win?'

'If the foxes are truly coming down the river, Silken,' Master Grey said grimly, 'then no one's going to win.'

Early the next morning, Sedge and Silken swam out to fish, a polite distance away from the camp. No one had said anything, but it still felt wrong to eat anything but plants in front of the beavers. It had been tricky fishing along their journey, ducking away down side streams, or hanging back behind the main party to gobble down hasty meals.

'That's another good reason for keeping otters and beavers apart,' Sedge pointed out to his sister. 'They already think we're fierce and strange, it would be worse if they were to see us fishing.'

Silken dived and came up triumphantly with a silvery fish in her jaws. She dragged it out on a muddy, sandy patch where the bank sloped into the water, and settled down to breakfast. 'Maybe,' she muttered thickly through a mouthful. 'But if our mother and Teasel and the other otters turn up today and they're just as suspicious and worried as Master Grey and the elders are, we'll never agree on anything. Wouldn't it be better if we ate together, even if we're eating different things? I mean, they do know that we eat fish. And that's better than thinking otters hunt beaver kits, isn't it?'

Sedge felt a fish move slowly past under the surface and darted after it, snapping it swiftly out of the water. He climbed out next to Silken and ate silently for a while. At last he said, 'Do you think they'll ever listen to each other?'

'Only if they're frightened enough of the foxes,' Silken told him sadly. Then she glanced round, peering downriver, the way they'd come the day before. 'Sedge! Look!'

'What?' Sedge peered round her. 'Oh . . .'

Slowly rounding a bend in the river was a strange craft, built of branches lashed together and piled high with bags and bundles. Otters swam on either side, pulling the raft with ropes clutched in their teeth, and a tall, light-furred otter stood at the stern, poling the craft along.

'The raft otters,' Silken whispered. She dropped her fish, fascinated, and Sedge stood up on his hind paws.

It had been the raft otters who had first shown Silken who she truly was. The raft had sailed past her while she was out foraging, and it had changed everything. Sedge knew how important that moment had been for his sister. But there was something else she didn't know – something just as important. 'Do you know who that is?' he muttered in her ear.

'The travelling otters,' Silken said impatiently. 'I saw them before, I told you.'

'No, I mean the tall one, the one poling the raft. With the greyish fur.'

Silken frowned at him. 'No. Why would I?'

Sedge swallowed and then slipped into the water, beckoning Silken after him. He had to tell her, now.

'That's Campion. That's our father.'

Silken crouched frozen on the bank, gaping at Sedge, until he turned back to beckon her again. 'Come on!'

Silken swam frantically after him. 'Why didn't you tell me?' she hissed.

Sedge ducked under the water, twirling in the cool dimness to let the river clear his thoughts. 'I didn't *not* tell you,' he tried to explain as he popped up again. 'It just didn't come up – and you call Master Grey your father.'

'Only because – well, because I thought for so long that he was!'

'Yes, but you love him, Silken. Anyone can see that. He's more your father than Campion has ever been.' Sedge sighed, and snorted bubbles. 'More of a father than Campion has been to *me* too. I've hardly seen him since I was a tiny cub.'

The raft was closer now, and the otters pulling on the ropes had seen Sedge and Silken. One of them signalled to Campion, and he jammed the pole hard down into the river mud, angling the raft towards them.

'Are you two from Greenriver Holt?' one of the raft otters demanded, clawing the rope away from her mouth. 'What are you doing all the way down here?'

'Yes we are.' Sedge nodded at her. 'But we're here with . . .' He hesitated, unsure how to explain. Would the raft otters be horrified? Surely they had to be used to trading and meeting with other creatures – more so than the holt otters, anyway. 'We're here with the beavers from the Stronghold,' he said at last. 'We're envoys. There's going to be a meeting, between the lodge and the holt, to discuss what to do if the mountain foxes come this far down the river.'

'Foxes!' The raft otter drew back sharply, the water rippling around her. 'Campion! Did you hear that?'

'I did.' The pale-furred otter looked over at the island and the pebbled bank where Sedge and Silken had been breakfasting. 'We're landing. Over there; we'll tie up to a couple of those oak trees. Take your rope, Iris.'

The otter bit hard on her rope again and guided the raft

towards the island. Sedge and Silken paddled ahead of her, wanting to get back to the island and out of the raft otters' way. They scrambled out on to the pebbles, and then up on to the higher part of the bank, watching as the crew steered their raft in.

There was a flurry of activity as the otters dragged the raft up on to the pebbles, secured the ropes, and flung a woven reed cover over the boxes and bundles. Sedge wondered about offering to help, but they all seemed to know exactly what they were doing, even the two small cubs whose job it was to fasten down the cover with neat little knots. They finished their work, and then they all paused and gazed up at Sedge and Silken, almost in unison.

Sedge tried to remember that he was there as an envoy from the holt, Lady Thorn's heir. He had responsibilities. He bowed his head slightly and said, as loudly and clearly as he could, 'Would you like us to take you to meet Master Grey, the leader of the lodge?'

'No,' growled Campion, leaping up on to the bank beside them. 'I want to talk to you two first. What's going on? You shouldn't be all the way down the river on your own. And foxes? What nonsense is that?'

The rest of the raft otters followed him, scrambling up the bank and settling around Sedge and Silken. The ones who'd been dragging the raft started to roll luxuriously in the grass, squeezing the water out of their fur and stretching their aching muscles, but still clearly listening to Campion and the two strange cubs.

'We're here because our mother sent us,' Sedge said, trying to sound dignified and older and not at all like a squeaky little cub. 'She's following with her counsellors and guards. We came ahead to visit the lodge. My sister lived there, until – until recently.' He finished with a stumble. The last time the raft otters had passed down the river was when Silken had seen them, back in the spring. Everything that had happened since then would be news. They must have seen the high waters, even if they were down at the river mouth, trading with the sea creatures – but they obviously didn't know anything about the flood at Greenriver Holt, or about Silken's return. Campion must still think that Silken had drowned as a tiny cub.

In fact, Sedge realised sadly, his father had no idea who either of them were. He supposed it wasn't that much of a surprise – he'd grown a lot, of course – but somehow he felt a father ought to know. He coughed a little, clearing his throat, and added, 'Our mother is Lady Thorn.'

The grey-furred otter said nothing for a moment, but the other raft otters exchanged glances and whispers.

'Isn't that . . . ?'

'So these two . . .'

'But I thought the sister was . . .'

Sedge sank his claws into the pale fur of his belly, so as not to twist his paws together. Silken was always telling him not to do that. 'I'm your cub, Sedge. This is my sister, Silken. You would have last seen her back before the Dark Spring, when she was known as Elderberry.'

'The river gave you back?' Campion whispered, gazing at Silken.

Silken stepped forward and nodded. 'I was washed up half drowned in a swan's nest, and taken in by the lodge. I – I didn't know what I was. I was so small, and the flood had swept away everything I knew.' She reached out a paw and laid it pleadingly on Campion's. 'I saw you,' she whispered. 'Back in the spring, when you came down the river past the Stronghold, when the water was so high. I was watching you, hidden by the bank of a stream. Until then, I'd never seen an otter. I thought I was one of the beavers. I'd grown up thinking that you were my enemy.'

One of the raft otters – Sedge thought it was Iris – chattered disgustedly, and Campion growled at her. 'We have no quarrel with the beavers. Especially if they cared for our cub.' He turned back to Silken, speaking softly once more. 'How did you find your brother?'

'He found *me*,' Silken said, with a proud look at Sedge, who was practically pulling his belly fur out in tufts by now.

'I heard the river birds singing Silken's song,' Sedge explained, stilling his paws. 'It was our song, she'd made it just for us. So I knew she couldn't have drowned. I ran away to find her.'

'And I had already left the lodge when I saw you and realised what I was. I had set out to find the holt, and the otters,' Silken added. 'We met along the river, a few days' journey from here.'

Sedge nodded, but added nothing. There was no way to describe the strangeness of that first meeting.

Campion gazed at them. 'I haven't been able to think of Greenriver Holt without remembering that little lost cub,' he murmured.

'Is that why you hardly visited?' Sedge asked, his voice very small.

Campion's eyes widened, and the fur around his neck stood up into tiny spikes. 'I suppose that was part of it,' he admitted. 'But . . . we raft otters find the holt strange, you know. The beauty and comfort is fascinating, to begin with, but then . . . all that sameness, day after day.'

The other raft otters nodded, and Sedge sighed, very quietly. Campion had been a stranger for so long that he'd never thought much about what he'd inherited from his father.

Perhaps this was why he'd wanted to disappear down the river in search of adventure. After all, only half of him was a sensible, stay-at-home holt otter.

'Still.' Campion bowed his head slowly to Sedge. 'I should have visited more, at least. It was wrong of me to disappear, I see that now.'

'This is all very nice, I'm sure,' muttered Iris. She was either Campion's second-in-command or just bad-tempered and not afraid to show it, Sedge couldn't tell which. 'But what about these foxes?'

Campion growled again, very low in his throat, but Iris squared up to him, even though she was only about two-thirds his size. 'All right, all right,' he grumbled. 'Though I don't know why you're fussing. There are no foxes anywhere close to this part of the river.'

'Seems strange that beavers and otters are bothering to hold a great meeting together about them then,' Iris snapped back. She turned on Sedge and Silken. 'Something they've certainly never done before. Unless you're making this up. Are you?'

'No!' Sedge's eyes widened. 'It's true, I swear. The old swan passed on a message to our mother. The foxes have been flooded out of their home den in the mountains, and now they're travelling downstream, ravaging all along the banks.'

Campion sniffed doubtfully.

'Lady Thorn wanted to meet with the lodge anyway though,' Silken put in. 'The river burst its banks earlier this spring, and after the flood, she wanted the holt to be more open. More generous.' She shifted uncomfortably, and admitted, 'Not everyone agrees.'

'I can imagine.' Campion looked quite shocked. The rest of the raft otters were whispering to one another again.

It did all sound strange, Sedge had to admit. Beavers. Swans. Cubs on their own, several days' journey away from the holt. No wonder the raft otters looked worried and uncertain.

'How far away is your mother?' Campion demanded.

'She must be close by now,' Sedge said, looking to Silken, who nodded her agreement.

'The new moon is tomorrow night,' she said. 'That's when the meeting is to take place.'

'They didn't start out until five days after us,' Sedge explained. 'We left earlier to give us time to reach the Stronghold, and bring the message to Silken's father, and then travel back here together.'

He realised what he had done as soon as the words left his mouth.

Silken's real father flinched, and Sedge added quietly, 'I meant her foster-father. That's Master Grey, the leader of the lodge.'

Silken nudged him comfortingly and said, 'Vane has promised to come too. He's the swan who first heard the rumours about the foxes.'

Campion shook himself, standing straighter again. 'I've seen that swan, and heard his name spoken. He has flown up and down this river many times, and much further afield too. We should listen to him. Even if it's news we don't want to hear.' He glanced up over Sedge and Silken's heads, and brushed his whiskers with one paw, as though he was amused. 'We have an audience,' he said, nodding at something behind the two cubs.

Sedge and Silken whirled round and saw Brindle, peeping round a slim birch trunk. He gasped as he realised that he'd been spotted and bundled away into the thick undergrowth.

'Eavesdropping!' Silken spat crossly. 'He'll be straight to his mother.'

Campion and the others looked curious, and Sedge sighed. 'Not all the beavers are keen on us working together. That kit's mother tried to lead an uprising against Master Grey, back at the lodge. She and her mate and kit are here to keep them out of trouble . . .'

Campion snorted and rubbed his paws together as though he was anticipating some delicious dish. 'This meeting is getting more and more interesting.' With a flourish, he swept into a low bow. 'I think it's time you introduced us to the beavers of the Stronghold.'

Sedge had assumed that when otters and beavers first met, there would be a grand and formal introduction. After all, it was the first time that they'd met properly, ever, as far as he knew. He had been expecting speeches, and his mother in a wreath and her best claw-guards, walking gracefully across the island accompanied by her tallest, grandest otters.

Instead, he and Silken were leading a band of swaggering, laughing raft otters to meet Master Grey. Otters that they didn't know, and certainly didn't trust – even if one of them was their own father.

The beavers were still putting the finishing touches to the shelters they'd built, now that it was daylight. Sedge was starting to learn that beavers never thought anything was actually finished, as there were always more improvements that could be made. He expected to see Tawny waiting for them, since surely Brindle would have warned her. But she was nowhere to be seen. Master Grey and several of the elder beavers were standing in front of one shelter that obviously hadn't stood up to the night's winds as it should, looking disgusted. One of them kicked it, and a branch rolled sadly to the ground.

'Um.' Sedge made a sort of coughing noise, and one of the beavers glanced back to see what was going on. Then he yipped, a sharp, surprised yelp that had Master Grey and the others turning round too. Silken's foster-father frowned at the group of otters – he had seen Lady Thorn before, and he clearly knew that these weren't the otters from Greenriver Holt.

'Master Grey, this is Campion, the leader of the travelling otter band. They were – um. They happened to be passing . . .' Sedge trailed off, looking at Campion to help him explain. The beavers knew of the raft otters, but only because they hid themselves away as soon as the watch spotted the raft passing along the river. Sedge was sure they'd never come this close, let alone spoken to each other. 'Campion, this is Master Grey, the master builder of the Stronghold.'

Campion bowed, this time without the smirk and the extravagant twirls. He actually looked respectful. 'Honoured, Master Grey.' He looked down at Silken and Sedge, and went on, 'The cubs are perhaps too shy to mention something else. It seems I owe you a great debt of thanks, for rescuing and raising my daughter.' He gestured to Silken, who gazed anxiously at her foster-father.

Master Grey was silent for a moment, but then he nodded to Campion – with no flowery bowing – and reached out to pat Silken's paw. 'We did badly by not returning Silken to her holt. I knew that she didn't belong to us. I didn't know how to find her real home, but I didn't try hard enough. We beavers shouldn't have kept ourselves apart for so long.'

'A fault of ours too,' Campion agreed politely, and the two sides gazed at each for a moment, everyone unsure what to say. The other beavers were gathering around the edges of the group now, staring at the otters in frightened fascination.

Sedge cast a worried sideways look at Silken, wondering what to do next. He felt responsible – as though it was up to him to make this work. The blood was thumping in his ears, louder and louder, until he realised that the sound wasn't inside him at all – there were wings beating overhead, and soon all the otters and beavers were looking up into the pale morning sky.

Vane was back. The old swan made a wild, splashing landing out in the river – just ahead of Lady Thorn and her court of otters, who were paddling downriver in close formation. Sedge watched their mother's eyes widen as she saw the raft otters there on the island. Her gaze fixed on Campion, and Sedge was sure he caught a glance of dismay flickering between her and Teasel. His mother hardly ever spoke about Campion,

Sedge realised. Wasn't that odd? Was the tall, grey otter no more to her than the father of her cubs? Teasel was more her mate than Campion had ever been, he realised, as he watched the grizzled old otter draw closer behind his mother.

Vane folded his wings and sailed slowly to the bank, with Lady Thorn swimming beside him, her head smooth and dark above the water. The otters scrambled out on to the shore, and Lady Thorn shook the water from her coat, nodding briefly to Campion and to Master Grey. She pulled Sedge close and nuzzled against him, and laid her paw on Silken's. Then she stood up, gathering everyone around with one long look.

'This should have been a grand day, full of speeches and songs and solemn meetings,' she said, her voice clear and sad. 'The first real meeting of the otters and the beavers. An opportunity for us to take time to overcome our fears and suspicions and build a new friendship together.' She shook her head. 'It's time we no longer have. Vane has news, my friends.'

The old swan hissed and mantled his wings above his back. 'Indeed. I flew upriver again when the otters set off for this meeting. I found the fox troop, closer than I saw them before. Closer to the holt.' There was worried muttering from the crowd and Vane looked solemnly around at them all. 'The foxes are coming.'

CHAPTER EIGHT

The threat of the foxes felt suddenly and terrifyingly real. Silken had hardly heard of foxes before the swan had told his story, and she hadn't known enough about them to be frightened. Teasel's story had scared her – but even then, the mountains had seemed so far away. The foxes might have moved out of their home, but surely they were never going to travel all that way down the river? Silken had seized on the story as a way to bring the otters and beavers together and visit her foster-father and her old friends. But now the foxes were no story. They were real and they were coming for the holt.

Their mother was with Master Grey, Vane and Campion in a tiny clearing among the oak trees, talking urgently. Meanwhile, everyone else waited. Silken found herself in the strange position of go-between, carrying cautious messages between the otters and the beavers, as well as tiny gifts – flowers, sweet herbs and a bright feather that one of the raft otters had found. Frost,

Speckle and Sedge were playing a game with pebbles and sticks and signs scratched into the mud, but they were only concentrating on it enough to argue about who was winning. Teasel was asleep, or at least pretending to be. Silken didn't see how anyone could sleep just now.

At last, Master Grey, Lady Thorn and Campion came walking slowly back towards the shelters, with Vane padding behind them. Silken dropped the little bundle of herbs she was carrying – she'd forgotten that she had them in her paws. Otters and beavers mingled together as they hurried to hear what had been decided.

'We otters will go back up the river at once,' Lady Thorn said, looking around at them all. 'Our holt has only just recovered from the spring floods – we can't risk an attack by foxes now.'

'And I have agreed – we beavers will help defend the holt,' Master Grey said. 'If the foxes take the otter holt, who's to say they won't send raiding parties on down the river and attack the Stronghold?' He looked lovingly at Silken. 'Besides, we are bound together now, with bonds of friendship and of family. We cannot let our own small otter be put at risk.' He glared around at the other beavers, looking fiercer than Silken had ever seen him. 'Does anyone have anything to say to that?'

There was silence.

'But – but *how* will we defend the holt?' Sedge asked, his voice a little shaky.

Teasel gave him a disapproving, cubs-should-be-seen-and-not-heard look, but then she said, 'The cub's only asking what everyone else wants to know.'

'We will talk to the foxes,' Lady Thorn said firmly, at the same time that Campion said, 'Fight,' and Master Grey said nothing at all.

That was not the end of the discussions, of course. The arguments went on late into the night, with beavers and otters stomping and grumbling around the fire. Lady Thorn seemed to be convinced that a polite embassy to the foxes would warn them away, whereas Campion and Teasel and several of the beavers thought there was no hope of that at all, and the only way to convince foxes of anything was a show of strength.

'I told you, they're vicious!' Teasel snapped, eyeing Frost and a couple of the other beavers irritably. 'And if their own den's been destroyed, as Vane says, they'll be angry, probably grieving their lost ones. They won't want to listen to sweet words from us!'

'So what are you suggesting then?' Frost asked. 'We can't

just storm up the river and attack them when they haven't done anything wrong!'

'You think we should wait for them to attack first?' Teasel snorted. 'Try explaining that to the mother of the cub they've killed. I've done that. You haven't.'

Frost fell uncomfortably silent.

'She knows what she's talking about, youngster,' Campion said gently to the young beaver. 'I've seen foxes on our travels, and you don't want to underestimate them. We need to travel back up to the holt as fast as we can and set a strong guard around it.'

'Not just a guard,' Master Grey rumbled. 'Fortifications too. We can help with that.'

Lady Thorn nodded gratefully. 'We would welcome your help. Even if the foxes never come down the river, it would be good to make the holt more defensible.'

Silken saw Campion and Iris exchange a glance. Clearly they thought that Lady Thorn was far too optimistic. 'While you're arming the holt,' Campion went on, 'we need to send a scouting force to keep a close watch on what those foxes are up to. If we get a chance, perhaps we *can* talk to them, but we need to know what they're planning. They've already attacked Vane, remember. His wing's still healing. They're fearsome creatures.'

'But that's what we thought about you,' Frost protested,

and Campion bared his teeth. But Frost stood his ground, only flattening his ears very slightly.

'Stop that,' Iris growled at Campion. 'Deliberately frightening young ones. Though he can be fearsome,' she added to Frost. 'Don't you cross him.'

'We already knew otters were fierce,' Speckle put in, sounding unimpressed. 'Sedge killed the old wolf, didn't he? And I bet she was a lot bigger than any foxes.'

Campion swung round to stare, and Sedge sighed inwardly.

'The night wolf? You?'

Did his father have to sound quite so surprised? He wasn't that small and feeble! 'Yes,' Sedge admitted. 'But it wasn't a fight. She was attacking Silken. I just crept up behind her and hit her with a rock.'

Campion looked delighted, if still a bit shocked. 'Cunning as well as brave. That answers that question then. You'll definitely be one of the scouts we take upriver.'

'And me!' Silken jumped up.

'If I'm going, then Silken should too,' Sedge agreed. 'She rescued me from the flood just before the wolf turned up.' He wasn't entirely sure that he wanted to go and fight foxes, or even just spy on them, but he definitely wanted to see more of the river. And if he was going, then he wanted Silken there with him.

'Both of you,' Campion agreed.

'No.'

Sedge had forgotten that his mother was there listening to all this, but she was suddenly facing up to Campion, so fierce and determined that he stepped back nearly into the fire. Her muzzle only came up to his shoulder, but it didn't seem to matter. 'You can't take both the heirs to the holt on a journey like that. What happens if – I've already lost Silken once! And when Sedge disappeared as well . . . I thought I'd never see either of my cubs again. I won't let you take them.'

'Then you come too!' Campion reached out to touch her muzzle, but Lady Thorn flinched away. Sedge saw the hurt in his father's eyes.

'Ma. Don't *we* get a say?' Sedge dropped the words into the silence, and his mother whirled round, staring at him. He pressed on anyway, guilty but determined. 'How could we ever claim we're worthy to lead the holt, either of us, if we don't go? We've agreed that this is the greatest threat the holt has ever faced, greater than the floodwaters, even. We can't just hide away and pretend that it isn't happening!'

Silken moved closer to their mother. 'Please,' she said. 'If you think reasoning with the foxes is worth trying, then we can at least help do that.'

Teasel snorted, but Lady Thorn stretched up to rest her

muzzle on top of Silken's head for a moment, tawny fur against red-brown. 'I *want* to reason with them,' she whispered. 'I want to hope that we can meet them, and know them – as we've started to know the beavers here! That it's only their strangeness that's making us frightened, that we just need to understand them better. I can't bear to go straight to fighting, without even trying to talk. But . . . I'm terrified that this scouting party is heading into real danger. I can't bear to lose you again.'

There was a moment's stillness and then a scuffling and an angry scream. 'So your cubs are too precious to risk, but you'll happily send our kits off to be slaughtered by foxes?' Tawny hurled herself across the clearing at Lady Thorn as the otters and beavers watched, frozen and aghast.

Sedge shoved his mother sideways, out of the path of the angry beaver, and Silken barged forward into Tawny, snapping at the soft fur under her chin. Tawny reeled away, dazed by the blow. As they watched in horror, she staggered and fell into the still-glowing fire, the embers singeing her coat.

Her mate Russet dragged her out of the flames, and Frost joined him, rolling her in the dirt and thumping at the sparks in her fur, while Tawny whimpered from pain and shock.

Teasel scooped up Lady Thorn, anxiously patting and stroking her fur as she pulled her back on to her paws.

'What – what happened?' Lady Thorn murmured dazedly, leaning into her companion's embrace.

'Tawny,' Silken spat angrily, but Sedge could see that she was shaking. He knew that all she'd meant to do was push Tawny away, not injure her. The smell of burnt fur was sickening.

'Are you hurt, Ma?' he asked worriedly. 'I'm sorry I pushed you like that. But she had this.' He slowly held up a stone blade, a sharpened flint that gleamed dully in the firelight, and the excited, nervous chatter around the fire died away into silent horror.

'An otter's knife,' Silken whispered. 'She must have stolen it . . . for this.'

'Murderer!' Teasel spat at Tawny, who now drooped between Frost and Russet. Frost looked down at her in disgust, as though he'd quite like to drop her again, but he put out a heavy paw to stop Teasel.

'Stay back, friend,' he rumbled. 'I wouldn't blame you, myself, but it isn't right. It's up to Master Grey to deal with her.'

'The first meeting between our kinds, and you came to kill, Tawny?' Master Grey shook his head. He looked weary. 'I should never have let you out of my sight after what happened at the lodge. We're here to build a peace between us all. You've shamed us.'

'I *fought* for us,' Tawny whispered, so faintly that they had to lean in to hear her. 'I'm fighting for my kit. I won't let Brindle grow up among such traitors.'

'You're the traitor,' Frost growled.

'It's you who have put your own kit in danger,' Master Grey told Tawny. 'And your mate. My elders told me I should banish you after you tried to overthrow me. But I couldn't imagine sending a young family out to fend for themselves. I wanted you and your mate to see that the threat we face is not the otters. I had no wish to exile you. Now I see no other option. After you're healed, there will no longer be a place for you at the Stronghold. Russet and Brindle will go with you.'

Russet nodded soberly. Sedge wondered whether Tawny had told him her plan or whether he had been as surprised as they were. It didn't matter – there was no point in protesting. Tawny had gone beyond what was forgivable now.

Tawny was led away to have her wounds tended, and Master Grey turned to Lady Thorn, who was still trembling. 'I am deeply sorry for this,' he said quietly.

'That's all very well,' Teasel said. 'But if you knew that she hated us, and she wanted no part in these talks, then you put us at risk when you brought her here.'

'I did,' Master Grey admitted sadly. 'I was foolish, and too trusting.'

Teasel stared at him in silence. Sedge thought that she'd been expecting him to protest, and now she didn't know what to say.

'I am so very ashamed, Lady Thorn,' Master Grey continued, bowing to her. 'That one of my own lodge should break the peace that we were starting to make. Beavers build, you see,' he said simply. 'I was hopeful that we could build something here that would last for ever.'

'Do not be ashamed,' Lady Thorn said. 'There are those within our holt who can't bear the thought of this meeting either. Not everyone agrees that we should be working together, even with the threat from the foxes.' She shivered. 'I can't promise that an otter wouldn't try to do the same thing.'

'Never,' Teasel muttered, but she didn't sound very confident.

'And Tawny was right,' Lady Thorn continued sadly. 'I would have been willing to let her kit join this journey upriver to spy on the foxes, while I huddled my cubs safely away in their holt.'

Sedge's chest tightened at the sadness in his mother's voice. But he couldn't damp down the excitement squirming inside him. 'So . . . we can go?'

Lady Thorn nodded. 'Yes. Things are changing for our holt. Whichever of you leads us one day, you'll need to know more about the river, and the creatures who live around her waters. I have to let you be part of this.' She looked up at Teasel, and then at Campion, standing with his raft otters gathered around him. 'You'll be there to watch over them for me, both of you?'

Teasel wrinkled her muzzle reluctantly, but she nodded, and Campion bowed to both of them. 'My otters will stand for our kind. And we will fight if we must.'

Master Grey sent a few beavers back down the river to let the lodge know that he would be travelling onwards with the otters. They carried Tawny with them on a raft, a small, rough craft that Campion's otters had made, which Iris said would probably last the journey back to the Stronghold. She sounded as though she wouldn't mind that much if it didn't, and Silken agreed with her.

At least Tawny's attack seemed to have gone a long way towards unifying the otters and the beavers – which was exactly the opposite of what she'd wanted. All the otters had witnessed how utterly horrified the beavers had been when they saw Tawny fly at Lady Thorn with a weapon. And they'd heard their lady of the holt admit that there were otters who felt the same way.

Everyone else set off back upriver, travelling as fast as possible. Silken was startled at how much more quickly they could cover the distance with the raft. Although the raft otters couldn't pole their craft quite as fast as an otter could swim, they were still fast – and most importantly, the holt otters and the beavers could rest. Silken was used to stopping for naps to build back up the energy she'd used on swimming. Now, with the raft otters taking turns to wield the pole and drag on the ropes, the journey back to the holt was quicker and easier than she and Sedge could have imagined. Even Vane stopped for an occasional nap on the raft, though he clearly found it strange to be poled along.

They were greeted joyfully by the otter guards posted along the river, but there was urgent news to pass on too. Lady Thorn had told the holt's lookouts to listen for the gossip along the riverbank from the birds and the smaller river creatures. It was something the otters had never tried to do before – they had always kept themselves separate. But Lady Thorn was determined that would change. Holt otters had given friendly greetings to passing waterbirds – most of them had hurried away in panic, but one or two had stopped to talk. Bramble had actually offered some of his fiercely guarded supplies to a family of hedgehogs whose home had been destroyed in the flood.

Even when they couldn't persuade the little animals to talk to them directly, the otters were making an effort to listen.

The finches and warblers and ducks were full of rumours about the foxes, and the chatter had only grown while Lady Thorn and her envoys were at Oak Island. All reports indicated that the foxes were on the move in large numbers, and travelling swiftly down the river towards them.

As Lady Thorn and the others swam up to the holt, Silken noticed that there were mice peering at them through the long grasses on the riverbank. She'd never seen that happen before, not in the time she'd been back at the holt, or in that strange, half-forgotten time before the Dark Spring. The holt had always been for otters, and otters alone. The willow tree had hardly ever had birds in its branches either. 'Look,' she whispered to Sedge now, nodding up at the swathes of green. Peering down at them was a greenfinch, the bright bands of yellow and green on its wings flashing among the leaves.

The tiny bird twittered nervously as it saw them watching, and Silken realised that it wasn't the only one. A whole flock of greenfinches was there in the tree, shrilling little comments to one another about the raft and Lady Thorn's return with the old swan from down the river, and the strange, furred creatures who were with the otters too – *and just what was going on with that, hmm? We will never understand these otters, never.*

Silken bowed politely to the crowd of birds, and Sedge

copied her, which prompted another chorus of fascinated twittering.

'Did you see that?' one of them asked, quite clearly, and Silken nudged Sedge in amusement.

Lady Thorn was leading the beavers ceremonially inside the lodge now, and the birds practically hung themselves upside down to watch – then they flew away in a riot of green and gold, clearly off to share this strange news.

'It's good to be home,' Silken said slowly, perching herself on one of the willow roots and looking around. The river level was back to where it should be now, the water calm but still swiftly flowing, and the early summer trees were heavy with rich green leaves. There was a cherry tree covered in pink and white blossom not far along the bank from the holt, and the flowers filled the air with sweetness.

'So it does feel like home to you now?' Sedge asked hopefully. 'I love exploring and travelling, but when I'm away, I miss the holt too.' He glanced away. 'I wasn't sure if you ever would.'

'I did miss it.' Silken nodded. 'It feels . . . right to be here. But I'm glad we travelled to the Stronghold. I had to go back, to understand how I felt about them both.' She sniggered. 'Tawny didn't exactly make me feel welcome though.'

'Perhaps there's a way that you can travel still,' Sedge said. He hesitated a moment, and went on, 'You could always travel with the raft otters. I mean, Campion is our father. I'm sure he'd let you.'

'Maybe.' Silken gazed at the raft, drawn tight against the bank and moored to a pair of slim silver birches. The covers had been stretched over the bags and boxes again, but it looked like they hadn't been tied down properly. The furthest corner was flapping. She nudged Sedge and nodded to it, and the two otters leaned forward, watching curiously.

A small dark paw appeared at the edge of the woven cover, feeling around as though its owner wasn't quite sure how close they were to the edge of the raft. Silken watched, holding her breath, as a blunt muzzle came next. A big black nose, a thick set of white whiskers, small round black eyes. A beaver. A beaver *kit*.

'Brindle!'

The kit froze, then looked around wildly.

'Get over here!' Silken snarled.

Brindle drooped and slunk miserably around the edge of the raft to hop on to the bank. He stood there in front of Silken and Sedge, his expression a strange mix of sulky and scared.

'What are you doing?' Silken demanded. 'You can't be here! You're supposed to be back at the Stronghold by now, with your mother and father!'

'Only until my mother's better,' Brindle snapped back.

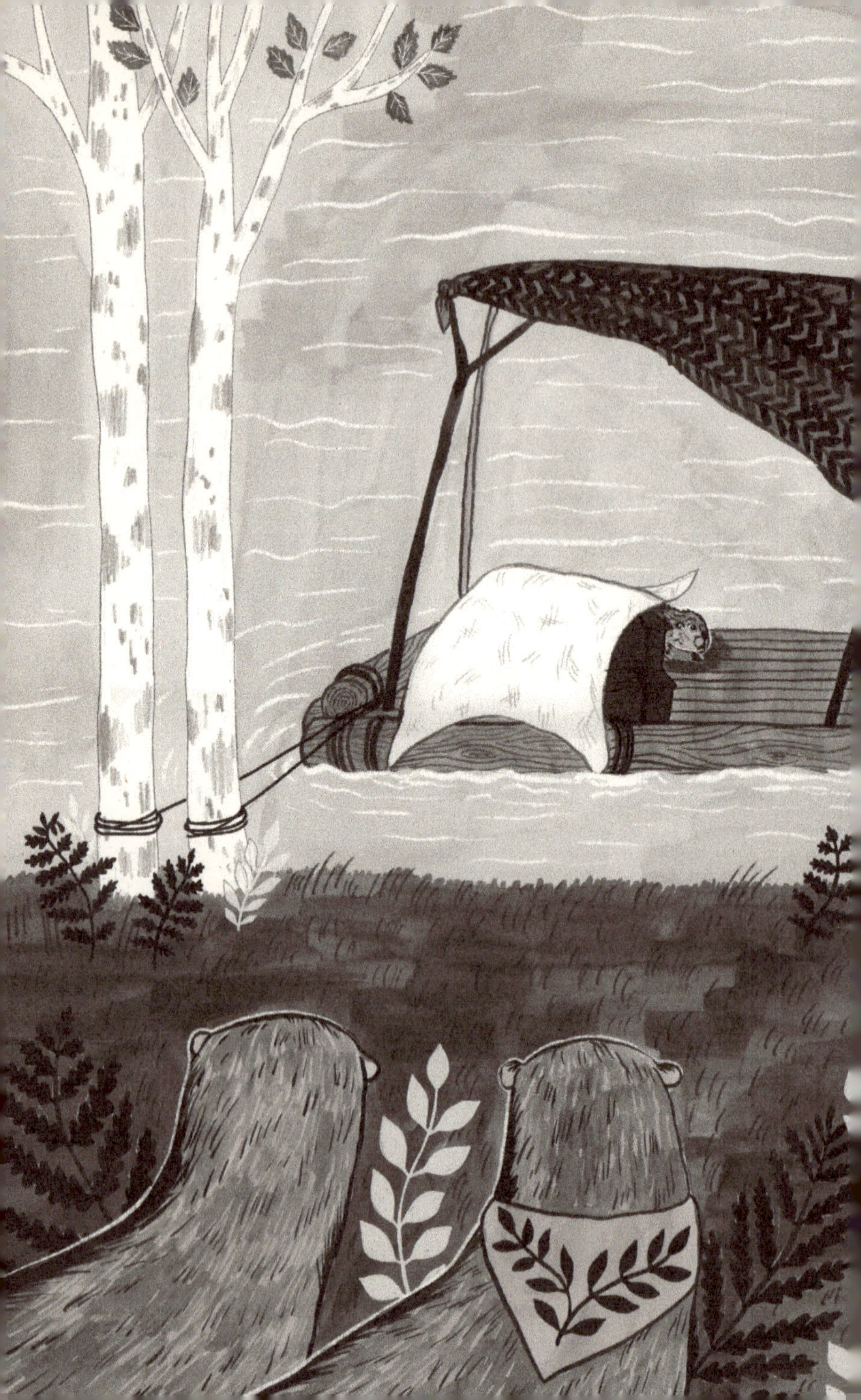

'You know, because she's burned all over from when you pushed her into the fire.'

Silken was silent for a moment. 'I never meant to do that,' she said at last. 'You know that, don't you?' She looked pleadingly at him. 'It was an accident.'

Brindle sighed. 'I know.'

'I don't understand how he's here,' Sedge whispered to Silken. 'He's only little! How did he—'

'I'm not that little,' Brindle interrupted with a growl. 'Just because I'm one of the youngest at the lodge everyone thinks I'm practically a newborn. I can hide between a couple of boxes without any help!'

'But you can't get out of them again without being spotted,' Silken pointed out sweetly, and Brindle hissed at her.

'I thought everyone had gone inside,' he said. 'Didn't know you two were still hanging around.' He scowled at them.

'You'll have been missed,' Silken said. 'Your mother's going to be panicking and telling everyone those murdering otters have kidnapped you.'

'Or we've turned you into a fur hat,' Sedge added, remembering what Silken had told him.

'My mother won't have noticed,' Brindle said bitterly. 'I've hardly spoken to her since we left the Stronghold. She's angry with me, because I told her she had to stop saying that she was scheming against Master Grey to protect me. It was all nonsense. And now she's injured as well. She was fevered. If she even misses me, she'll just think I've gone off somewhere to sulk again.'

'Wait, you mean you never wanted to be part of her plot to overthrow Master Grey?' Sedge blinked at him.

'I didn't know anything about it.' Brindle shuffled his paws, looking embarrassed. 'I slept through it. The whole thing. I would never have helped her, never!'

Silken nodded slowly, thinking back. 'You weren't there . . . I hadn't realised.'

'What about your father?' Sedge asked.

'I told him I was leaving,' Brindle said quietly. 'He said I was right to go. He'll be banished with my mother – he said he had to be, Master Grey was only being fair. And he couldn't bear to stay at the lodge and have everyone look sideways at him for ever and a day. If I went back with them, I'd have had to go into exile too. But I thought if I joined the expedition against the foxes, maybe I could prove I was loyal? Or even if I can't do that . . . I didn't think Master Grey would send me into exile on my own. I hoped he might just let me stay . . .' He didn't sound very sure.

'They aren't going to leave you all on your own, that's for sure.' Silken wrinkled her muzzle, thinking of Russet, exiled from his lodge for ever.

Brindle wriggled nervously, and Silken sighed. 'We can't leave you here at the holt. Not after your mother just tried to knife ours. Even though we're all supposed to be friends and allies, that's not going to go down well with the rest of the holt, is it? No, you're going to have to come with us on this scouting expedition.'

Brindle nodded eagerly, and Silken frowned at him. 'Have you been hidden between those boxes all the way up the river?'

Brindle nodded again.

'So you haven't eaten anything all that time?' He did look very small and skinny for a beaver kit. He was all fur and not much underneath.

'I did sneak a little bit of bark that Frost had left,' Brindle admitted. 'I was so hungry.'

Sedge snorted with laughter. 'He had a proper argument with Speckle about that. It was his midnight snack. He swore she must have eaten it.'

'Come on.' Silken beckoned to the kit. 'We'd better take you somewhere you can do some foraging.' She glanced over her shoulder at the holt as they hurried away between the birch trees. 'Too many guards around here.'

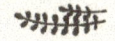

There didn't seem to be a lot of point in revealing their stowaway before the scouts left the holt again. Far better to hide him until they were too far from the holt to have to take him back, Sedge and Silken decided.

For now, they hid Brindle back between the boxes, with a large store of foraged birch bark. Sedge was slightly horrified that was all he wanted, but Silken and Brindle promised him that it would be fine.

The scouting party stayed only one night at the holt – the rumours coming down the river about the foxes were urgent enough to send them on their way at once. From the information the birds were bringing, the foxes were hardly more than three days' swim away – although it would likely still be a longer journey for them, travelling on foot.

Now it was clear that the foxes were a real danger, there were far more otters willing to join the expedition as scouts. Teasel had recruited twenty of the otters who usually acted as guards for the holt, and all the raft otters were keen to go too, with only the two smallest staying behind. Teasel and Campion would lead them all upriver with one of the elder beavers, Sandy, who was known for her wise words. Master Grey was hoping that she could negotiate with the foxes if they came close enough. For now, the scouting party was to head to the borders of the otter territory. There was no wall, nor any kind of border mark, but the otters – and everyone else on the Greenriver – had always known that two days' journey up and down the river was their water. It had been that way for ever. But no one had needed to tell that to a bunch of marauding foxes before.

If the foxes came creeping into the holt's territory, *something* would have to be done. Even if they settled on the borders, they could come hunting and foraging into the otter lands, and that would be worrying enough. The otters and beavers would make a stand at the edge of the holt's waters – but no one seemed to be able to tell Sedge and Silken what would happen next. Sorrel the healer was travelling with the scouting party though, which gave Sedge a cold feeling inside. Did Campion and Teasel think that they would need him? What were they really heading into? And now he and Silken were bringing a beaver kit along too, one even younger than themselves.

They set off early the next morning, a large party with the raft at its centre. The river narrowed up above the holt, becoming faster and wilder. The raft was harder to manage, and Sedge realised how skilled the raft otters were at poling their craft, Campion especially. They had to fight the raft over rapids, and it bounced and leaped so much that the young otters worried about Brindle, tucked away between the boxes.

After a day's long swim, the banks changed too. The trees were heavier and darker, clustering thickly along the river's rocky margins, and the lush grass had given way to scrubbier patches between boulders. As they swam, they noticed creatures along the banks stopping curiously to watch them – there were no beavers this far up, Sandy told them. The raft otters didn't usually come this far either, since there were no more otters this way along Greenriver to trade with. No one had ever seen a procession quite like this before.

'Hey there!' Campion called to one large rabbit, who was watching them from behind a tuft of long grass. He dug the pole down into the riverbed to hold the raft still, and everyone paused, some of the otters scrambling out on to the sunny rocks to stretch and sunbathe and squeeze the heavy, chill water out of their coats.

The rabbit looked behind her anxiously, as if she wasn't sure Campion was actually talking to her. She was on full alert, Sedge realised, her ears pricked straight up. He climbed out of the water close by her and on to a rock. She had very big eyes, he noticed, which were set on either side of her head, so she could see all around and easily spot anything that might be creeping up on her. They flickered nervously.

'We only want to talk to you,' he promised, looking down at her, and the rabbit nodded, her head still twitching from side to side as she tried to keep all the otters and beavers in view. Sedge got the impression she'd like to run for her burrow, but she didn't quite dare. Campion gestured at Sedge to continue, since the rabbit seemed to be listening to him, and Sedge gulped and lowered his voice to sound gentler. 'Were you looking at the raft? That's my father over there poling it along. Campion. He's an otter. We're travelling up the river, because we've heard a lot of rumours about a band of foxes . . .'

The rabbit shuddered violently, and her hind feet twitched as though she was preparing to make a run for it.

'Oh, please don't go!' Sedge begged her. 'We don't know a lot about the foxes, you see, and we thought you might know. Have you heard about them, maybe?'

The rabbit hunched down a little and whispered, 'They're not here yet. But they're coming! Cousins have seen them.'

'Ask her how far,' Campion called quietly to Sedge, who nodded.

'That's very helpful,' he told the rabbit. 'We're most grateful to you. Would you know how far away they were, when your cousins saw them?'

'Our cousins in Pine Tree Warren saw the fox scouts two bends round the river from here. Out hunting for – for us! And for places to sleep.' She shook her ears wildly, squeaked and dashed away between the trees.

'Thank you!' Sedge called after her. He looked back at Campion and the others. 'That sounds close . . .' He swallowed. 'Are they – are they in holt territory already?'

'Two bends round the river,' Campion muttered. 'Last time I explored this far up was a while ago, but I'd say that's no more than a morning's swim. Yes.' He nodded grimly. 'It sounds as if they've crossed the borders already. Keep your eyes open, all of you, and be ready for the scent too.' He glanced at Sandy and Teasel. 'We keep going until we know they're close, yes? And then we'll see what happens. It's likely they've caught our scent already. We may need to send a messenger. A go-between.'

'What do foxes smell like?' Silken whispered worriedly to Sedge. 'I don't know what I'm trying to smell . . .'

'Strong,' Teasel growled to her. 'Strong and musky. You'll know it. It'll choke you.'

Sedge settled lower into the water, only his nose and eyes peeping out, and felt Silken draw closer so that they were swimming side by side, just far enough away that they didn't tangle their paws.

'Foxes and wolves are similar, aren't they?' Silken murmured. 'I mean, foxes are a lot smaller, of course. And I only know about one wolf, although I suppose there must be more . . .'

'Foxes are smaller, but I think they den together, like we do,' Sedge agreed. 'So even if they're smaller you get a lot of them at once.' He felt the water ripple as Silken shivered, and he leaned over to nudge her comfortingly with his nose.

'It feels wrong to be swimming closer and closer to them,' she said. 'That rabbit was so frightened.'

'I think rabbits are frightened of everything,' Sedge pointed out. 'But I know what you mean.'

'Stop!' One of the otter guards swimming out in front of the exploring party pulled up short in the water and swung round with a paw upraised. His nostrils flared as he sniffed the air. 'Yes,' he whispered. 'I smell them. It must be them. I've never scented this before.'

'There, look. Between the rocks,' Teasel hissed. 'It's scouting.'

It was only a swift glimpse of orange-red fur, but they all saw it – and then the vanishing of a white tail-tip as the fox hurried away, presumably to pass on news of these strangers travelling up the river.

Strangers. Enemies. Prey?

CHAPTER NINE

'So you just want to walk up to their camp?' Teasel spat disgustedly. 'That's your plan?'

'I don't see what other choice there is.' Sandy rubbed a paw over her ears, looking weary. 'We can't expect them to come to us – or not in a way we'd want, anyway. Someone has to make the first move, and I'd rather it was us. Me.'

Silken glanced around the little camp they'd made – pressed up against the river on one side, since foxes didn't swim – or at least they *hoped* foxes didn't swim. The night had seemed to creep up on them more swiftly here among the pine trees. Iris had made a fire, and it crackled and spat with pine sap, flaring up and hissing and making them all jumpier than ever. It was hard not to see red-brown fur in the sudden flashes of flame. Silken had to keep telling herself that it was the fire snarling, not angry foxes.

'I don't see why it should be a beaver,' Campion argued. 'It's holt territory they're in. It's the holt they're probably aiming to attack! The otters will be hit first if these foxes keep travelling downstream. One of us should go.'

Sandy shook her head. 'We don't know much about foxes, but all creatures seem to respect age. I don't have a lot else to recommend me, but I'm the oldest here. We may as well make use of that.'

'An otter should go with you then,' Campion replied, with a sigh.

'I'll go. I'm not sending any other otters into this.' Teasel looked grim, and Silken reached out a paw to her without meaning to, remembering that awful story Teasel had told about Blossom and the foxes. She must be dreading meeting them again. 'Don't fuss,' Teasel growled, but it was one of her gentler growls, almost friendly.

'We'll set out at first light.' Sandy brushed her paws together briskly. 'So. Has anyone managed to find some supper?'

They slept fitfully that night, huddled together around the fire, with someone on watch throughout the darkness. Foxes were night creatures, or so the rumours went, busiest at dawn and dusk.

Everyone was awake in the grey daybreak as Teasel and

Sandy brushed down their fur and prepared to set off along the riverbank to find the foxes' camp. Sedge and Silken went fishing after they'd left, not so much because they were hungry as for something to do. But all too soon they spotted the two elders stomping back along the bank.

'What did they say?' Campion demanded, galloping to meet them. Sedge and Silken popped out on to the bank, Silken with a fat chub dangling forgotten from her jaws.

'Nothing,' Teasel growled. 'They wouldn't talk to us.' She sounded fierce and angry, but there was a tremble in her voice. Silken thought she'd never looked older.

'But they're there? You saw them?' Sedge asked. 'Are there – are there lots of them?'

'A good many, it seems. Perhaps fifty or so. But we didn't get close enough for a proper look. They chased us off.' She looked round the circle of otters and beavers, and beckoned to Sorrel. 'They threw stones at us. Sandy is hurt.'

There were hisses of worry as everyone realised that the elderly beaver was nursing one front paw, holding it close against her fur. Sorrel hurried forward at once, murmuring tenderly as he examined the dangling paw.

'I don't think it's broken,' he said at last. 'Just badly bruised.'

'They threw stones?' Frost asked, his voice deep and angry. 'When the two of you were only asking to talk?'

Teasel slumped down by the ashes of the fire. 'We hardly saw them. I called out, and there was a rustling – I think they must have been watching us for a while, they were all concealed in the bushes, so we caught only glimpses. Then a hail of stones.' She shook her head slowly. 'I don't know what we do next. If they won't talk . . .'

'We double the guard,' Campion said sternly. 'Keep trying to talk to them, but send messengers back to the holt too, at all speed. We need everyone able-bodied up here, ready. Then we watch for them to come to us. With more than stones.'

Teasel sighed. 'You think they'll attack? What about the defences Lady Thorn and Master Grey are building at the holt? Maybe we should fall back and make use of them.'

'But that practically begs the foxes to follow us down the river.' Campion flexed his claws and buffed them thoughtfully against his belly fur. 'Isn't it better to make our stand here, well away from the holt? There are older otters there, and cubs. Little ones . . . We should face them here and make it known they're not welcome further along the river. Then the foxes might not even want to come any closer to the holt. Perhaps they'll just decide to stay and make their home here peacefully.'

Silken abandoned the silvery fish, dropping it in the grass. She hadn't been hungry, anyway. Was Campion really suggesting that they let the foxes take this part of the riverbank? 'But – this is holt territory,' she said helplessly. 'They can't just arrive and say it all belongs to them now!'

Sandy waved her injured paw, and Sorrel, who was trying to bandage it up, tutted crossly. 'Try telling them that.'

'I suppose . . .' Silken whispered sadly. It seemed so strange, and it made her wonder. Who had lived by the old willow tree, she wondered, before the otters had decided to make it their home? Had they driven away a family of mice, or rabbits, all that time ago?

Campion spoke into the silence. 'So, do we stay or do we retreat back to the holt? Are we ready to fight here, if the foxes attack?'

'Of course we are,' Iris snapped. 'That's what we came for. To chase them back into the mountains.'

'We came to talk,' Sandy said softly. She bowed slightly to Sorrel, who had finished tying the bandages. 'Thank you. That feels much better.' She looked around them all, consideringly. 'But now that talking seems impossible . . . if we are to stay and make a stand, what about these younger ones?' she asked Campion. 'Our Frost and Speckle, and your two cubs. They're too young to fight.'

'What?' Frost bounced forward, showing his teeth. 'I'm twice your size!'

'It's our holt,' Sedge put in quickly. 'We can't sit by while everyone else fights for it. Our mother knew we might have to fight, and she let us go – even if she wasn't happy about it.'

Silken tugged him aside while the others argued. 'We have to tell them about Brindle,' she whispered. 'We can't risk leaving him hidden on the raft, not now. What if he comes out of hiding just when the foxes are attacking? Or what if – if he ends up all on his own . . .' She swallowed, her voice suddenly dry and squeaky.

'What are you two plotting?' Teasel said, with a suspicious glare. 'Whatever Lady Thorn said, you aren't going to be in the front of the fight, so don't even try arguing with me about it.'

'It's not that,' said Silken. 'We're happy to be scouts or messengers or help Sorrel with the healing. But the thing is . . .' She looked at Sedge, who sighed and nodded. 'The thing is, we aren't the only younger ones here.'

'Frost and Speckle, yes,' Teasel said impatiently.

Silken shook her head. 'There's someone else. Wait here.'

She darted away to the bank and slipped into the water, swimming round the raft to the loose edge of the cover where Brindle was hiding. She could hear the irritated muttering back on the bank as Sandy and Teasel demanded to know what was going on.

'Come on,' Silken called quietly under the raft cover. 'It's time to tell them you're here. It'll be all right,' she added, trying to sound reassuring.

'No, it won't,' Brindle growled, but he wriggled out from under the cover anyway and followed Silken back to the bank.

'Brindle!' Frost said, as they climbed back up the edge of the bank. 'He's not supposed to be here!'

Silken rolled her eyes at him. 'We know!'

Sandy stared at the small beaver, horrified.

'What have you done?' Teasel hissed angrily.

'We found him,' Sedge explained quickly. 'He's been stowed away on the raft.' He shrugged, holding up his paws. 'What were we supposed to do?'

'You were supposed to send him home!' Teasel snapped.

Silken scowled at her. 'How? We didn't find him till we were already at the holt. We were days away from his parents by then.'

'But now you've brought him into a battle!' Sandy said. 'Why didn't you leave him at the holt?'

'All on his own with a holt full of angry otters?' Silken stamped one paw. 'When his mother had just tried to knife the lady of the holt? How do you think that one would have gone?'

'Better miserable at the holt than killed by foxes.' Sandy

rubbed her good paw over her muzzle wearily. 'Now what do we do?'

'You should be asking *me*! I brought myself here!' Brindle marched over to her, furious. 'Why does no one ever talk to me?'

Sandy looked quite taken aback.

'I was the one who decided to hide on the raft.' He nodded at Campion, whose eyes were glittering. Her father looked almost as if he was enjoying this, Silken thought. 'I'm sorry. It was deceitful. But I didn't want to be exiled with a traitor.'

'We'll be taking care to check our cargo properly, from now on,' Campion told him. 'But you did well to stay hidden so long.'

Brindle ducked his head. 'I was so hungry that I sneaked out at the holt. That's when Silken and Sedge found me. I won't let that happen again.'

'Again? There is no *again*.' Sandy sighed. 'You're not staying here. Don't you understand the danger we're all in?'

Brindle nodded. 'I was there on Oak Island, I heard everything about the foxes. We have to stop them, we don't have any choice about it. I can help now I'm here. Anyway, where do you want me to go?' He looked slyly at Sandy. 'Off into the river on my own?' His voice quavered a little. Silken, watching him, thought it was entirely fake. He would have learned to do that sort of thing, she guessed, living with Tawny.

It worked on Sandy. The old beaver rubbed her muzzle again, and murmured, 'No, no, of course not.'

'Shut up, all of you,' Iris suddenly hissed. 'Quiet. Listen.'

Campion swung round, staring in the direction she was. All the guard otters from the holt straightened up, listening hard, their eyes sharp. There was a moment of frightened stillness, and then Campion gestured to Sedge, Silken and Brindle. 'Be careful, you younger ones. Stay close to the water's edge ready to swim for it if this doesn't go our way. You too, Sandy; you're in no shape to fight today.' He looked at Frost and Speckle. 'You two aren't much older than my cubs, as far as I can tell. I don't know when beavers learn to fight, but don't take any risks.'

'No one's stopping me,' Frost growled.

'Or me,' Speckle agreed, even though her voice was shaking.

Silken grimaced at Sedge. Neither of them knew much about fighting – Sedge had fought Lily's brother Pebble once and practically drowned, but that was all. This would be fighting on land too, where otters were at a natural disadvantage. But they didn't want to be left out.

'You three can help me to start with,' Sorrel said, appearing beside them as Campion and Teasel sent one of the guard otters back downriver to alert the holt. 'Sedge, show Brindle how to organise the supplies so that we're ready. Keep your eyes on me, in case I call for you to help with the injured.' He eyed them grimly. 'Don't try to do anything stupidly brave. Just because you've managed it once, Sedge . . .'

'I know. That wasn't me – it was luck,' Sedge muttered. 'Sorrel, look. I – I can see them.' He pointed across to the line of dark pine trees, and Sorrel sucked in a breath. Silken felt something squeeze in her guts as she caught a glimpse of red-brown fur dashing between the trees. It was far too late to retreat to the holt now, even if they'd wanted to.

There was a moment of stillness – and then the nightmare began.

The foxes erupted into the clearing in a wailing mass of teeth and fur and claws. They seemed to be everywhere, hundreds of them. Despite her brave words about wanting to fight, Silken found herself scurrying closer to Sedge, watching as otters and beavers hurled themselves into the fray.

'What can we do?' she whispered to Sorrel, who was staring intensely at the knots of fighting creatures.

'There! Follow me, you three.' The healer pointed to a soft mass of fur slumped at the edge of the clearing and darted swiftly through the crowd.

They hurried into the trees, weaving between them and staying out of sight as much as possible until they could reach the injured fighter. As they hurried by, Silken saw Frost fling himself against a huge fox, with Speckle close behind.

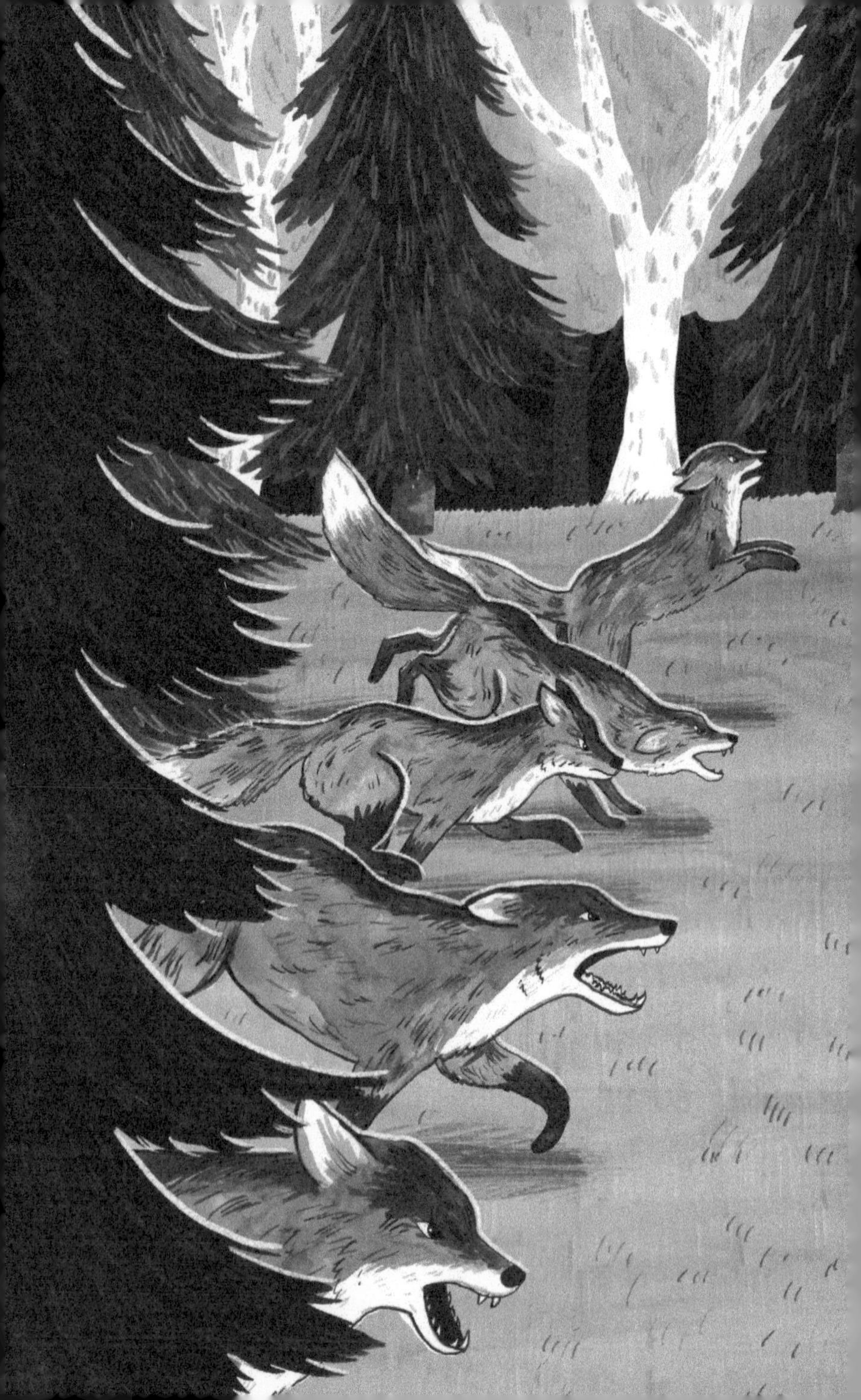

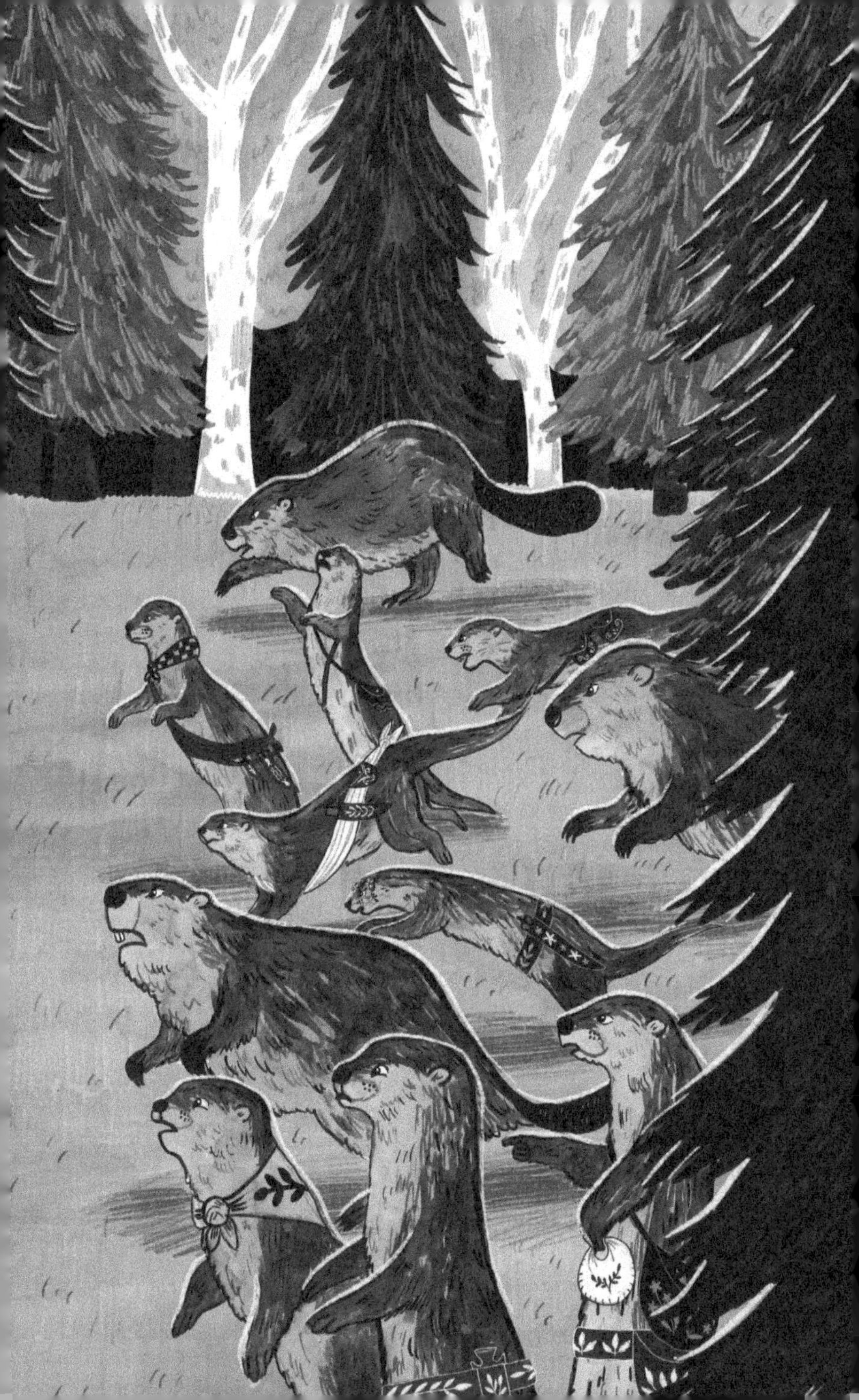

The otter was starting to stir a little as Sorrel crouched down beside him, and the healer hushed him gently. 'We need to carry him away from here,' he told his helpers. 'Back to the water's edge, where I can clean his wounds and bandage him up. It's not safe here.'

'But won't we make it worse by moving him?' Brindle whispered, looking at the jagged tear just above one front leg. He kept swallowing, clearly sickened by the dangling skin and seeping blood.

'Probably,' Sorrel agreed, tying a rough bandage around the wound. 'But we can't stay here, and we can't leave him. So he'll have to be carried.' He leaned down to the otter. 'Flag, listen to me. We're taking you to the river, but it's going to hurt you to be moved, I'm sorry. Swallow this for me – it will ease the pain.' He opened up a clay jar from his bag and tipped a dose of thick, dark liquid into the side of Flag's mouth.

'Was that willow bark?' Sedge asked, carefully packing the jar away and picking up the bag. Silken glanced at him, impressed. He'd told her that Sorrel was training him to have a little healer knowledge, but she hadn't expected him to know what he was doing among all this madness and mess.

'Yes,' Sorrel said in a low voice. 'It'll take a while to make any difference. Still. Sometimes it helps anyway. Now. We need to carry him as smoothly as we can.'

The four of them lifted Flag – a tall, full-grown otter – and staggered through the trees towards the water. He was only half conscious, and he sagged heavily between them, groaning as they stumbled over tree roots and jarred his wound.

When they got back to the water's edge, Sorrel laid Flag down. 'Brindle, gather me some bracken for a bed,' he rapped out. 'Silken, you go back to the clearing and watch. Call me when I'm needed. Sedge, you stay here with me.'

Silken didn't want to be there looking at what was under Flag's fur, but she envied Sedge his job. She hated watching the fight, even though she knew someone needed to. All around her were flashes of violence, sharp moments of terror and blood and darkness. She saw her father roll over and over with a grizzled fox, both of them snapping and hissing and clawing.

'Don't worry,' Sandy murmured to her. The old beaver was standing watching the fight, clutching a clay cup of water for any exhausted warrior that needed it. 'All that work on the raft has made your father very strong.' She seemed to be right – as Silken watched, the fox wriggled out of Campion's grip and limped away into the trees, head hanging. Her father shook his head wearily, and leaped back into the fight, flinging himself at a band of foxes who were menacing a beaver. Silken gasped as she realised that the beaver was Frost.

'Fetch the healer!' Campion roared at her, raking his claws

across the muzzle of one of the foxes. 'Fetch him now, Silken!'

Silken turned and dashed away, tumbling over the edge of the bank in her eagerness to grab Sorrel. 'You have to come! Frost's injured!'

'Stay here with Flag,' Sorrel told Sedge, galloping past her.

As they scrambled back up the bank towards the battle, they saw Campion already leading Frost across the clearing. The beaver was walking, but he looked dizzy, shaking his head confusedly from side to side. There were patches of fur torn away all over him, and Silken could see several deep gouges.

'We're chasing them off, I think,' Campion panted. 'Can you take him? Here. I need to get back.'

Silken watched him go, biting anxiously at her claws as she noticed his slight limp. She was so caught up in watching her father that she never saw the golden-bright fox leaping towards her. There was only the sudden panicked jolt as Sorrel threw himself in the way – and the fox's teeth snapped closed around his neck.

Sedge looked up anxiously at the scuffling of paws. He had been busying himself checking Flag's bandages. Sorrel must be coming back with Frost.

The huge beaver came stumbling over the rocky bank towards him, and Sedge stood up, reaching out to help. Then he stopped still. Following Frost were Speckle, Campion, Sandy and Silken – and they were carrying Sorrel. The healer hung between them, a loose bag of bones and fur, his head drooping.

'Sedge, you have to help him!' Silken gasped out. She was staggering under Sorrel's weight, and she sighed with relief as the four of them laid the healer down on one of the piles of bracken. Brindle coaxed Frost to sit down on another.

Sedge gazed helplessly at Sorrel's wound – a huge gash across his neck that had covered half his coat in dark blood. It needed cleaning and stitching, that was clear. But he'd never stitched a wound before! He'd watched Sorrel stitch up Flag, and had seen him work on one of the cubs back at the holt who'd caught himself on a sharp rock – but that was nothing like this.

There was no one else, though. He was Sorrel's pupil, and he was all they had. 'What happened?' he asked, as he grabbed a cleansing salve out of Sorrel's stores. 'He wasn't even fighting . . .'

'A fox was coming for your sister,' Campion said. 'Sorrel took the attack instead.'

'Please help him, Sedge,' Silken whispered. 'I didn't even see . . . The fox came out of nowhere.' She shuddered.

Sedge nodded, wiping carefully at the wound – and then

less carefully, as more and more blood came seeping out and speed seemed all that mattered. He had to get the stitches in. Sedge had sewn up old books in his lessons with Teasel, but stitching dried reed paper was nothing like pushing a needle through warm skin. And there was Frost behind him too, still dizzily shaking his head, and Flag moaning piteously on his bed of bracken. He couldn't do this!

'Stay and help your brother,' Campion ordered Silken, beckoning the others to follow him back to the fight. Sedge found himself alone with Silken and three creatures who were suddenly all his to care for.

'I've never stitched someone back up,' he muttered to Silken, taking up the needle and thread. 'I could kill him! I don't know what I'm doing. Here, can you hold this?' He handed a clean cloth to Silken, showing her how to press her paw against the wound.

'There's so much blood,' Silken whispered.

'I know. I know. How much has he got left to lose?' Sedge was stitching frantically through torn skin and muscle. But it was a jagged wound, the skin laced with toothmarks. He could feel Sorrel's life seeping out of him.

'Sedge,' Silken said quietly. 'Stop.'

'I can't,' Sedge muttered, intent on his work.

'It's no good. Not now. Look at his eyes . . .'

Sedge glanced up. 'What? Did the fox claw his eyes too? I don't know much about healing eyes. Is there eyebright, in that satchel?' He stared around wildly, and then at last he looked at Sorrel's face.

The healer's eyes were dark, and blank. The clear amber light that had shone out of them was gone. Sedge sat back on his paws and stared, remembering Sorrel happily instructing him on elderflowers, how to make paper out of reed stems, and a hundred other things that Sedge had probably wished he'd stop wittering about at the time. He would give anything to hear Sorrel telling him all about the benefits of eyebright again.

'He's gone, isn't he?' Silken asked, her voice a wisp.

'I haven't finished stitching him up,' Sedge muttered dully. 'I haven't finished.'

'Silken,' Brindle said behind them, sounding frightened. 'Sedge? You need to . . .'

Not Frost as well? Sedge whirled round in panic. In the horror of Sorrel's injury, he'd forgotten about Frost and Flag. But Flag was curled peacefully in the bed of bracken now, and Frost was sitting up, gazing at another otter who had clearly just stepped out of the river. Drops of water fell from her silver-white fur.

She paced slowly towards Silken and Sedge on all fours.

Her dark eyes were fixed on Sorrel's body, and while they held a look of sadness, there were sparks of anger deep down inside them. 'This should not have happened,' she said, her voice clear. 'This is wrong. This fight must stop. None of you should be warring like this. The taint of it is poisoning the river.'

'Will you look after him?' Sedge asked her pleadingly. 'He looked after everyone else. He died saving my sister.'

'He will be safe with me,' Lady River told him, and she wrapped one paw around Sedge's neck and pulled him towards her in a rough embrace. The touch of her fur made him shiver, but her breath was warm in his ear. 'I knew he was there, healing my otters. Exploring up and down my banks and harvesting the herbs and water plants. Loving me. I watched him, and he made my heart glad. He should have lived long, and passed on all that knowledge to you and the other young otters. This is wrong.'

'Can't you . . . change it?' Silken whispered.

Lady River turned to stare at her, and Silken cowered away. 'I can't,' the white otter told her gently. 'I wish I could. He's gone, and I can't bring him back. But you can stop the fighting. You must. No more dying.'

'Us? We can't stop it!' Sedge told her, but the white otter just shook her head.

'You must.' She turned to urge Silken forward and gently

patted a paw against her muzzle. 'You made them stop fighting at the lodge, don't you remember? *All those living by the river, we all now belong together.* You sang it so clearly.'

She ran one pale paw over Sedge's fur, and then she walked back towards the river, stopping to whisper softly in Flag's ear, and to nudge noses with Brindle and Frost, who were gazing at her in awe. She slipped away, disappearing like a strand of silvery foam on the water, leaving Sedge and Silken with Sorrel's body, and the news to break.

'She said you had to stop the fighting,' Brindle said stubbornly.

'Yes, but I wish she'd told us how,' Silken sighed. 'We can't just stop, can we? That means letting the foxes win.'

Sedge shook his head wearily. The otters and beavers had forced back the foxes – but it was only a temporary respite. Sedge had managed to patch up the rest of the wounded. There had been no more serious injuries, but he still felt hollow inside. Lady River had briefly soothed away a little of his sadness, but that hadn't lasted. He couldn't stop seeing Sorrel's empty eyes, even though he'd closed the soft lids over them himself.

'I saw her,' said Frost dreamily. He'd been dazed for hours

after the fight, and he was still moving slowly. 'Everything was hazy. But I knew her. She was the one who came to the lodge, when Silken sang to us that night of the rebellion against Master Grey. If she says we need to stop the fighting, then that's what we do.'

Sedge glanced at the main crowd of otters and beavers over by the fire. Campion and Teasel and Sandy were planning a counter-attack against the foxes. They meant to go in hard while the enemy were still exhausted from the day's fighting. They were planning to send out scouts to find ways to creep up on the foxes' camp and take them by surprise. No one was admitting that they were just as tired as the foxes were.

There was so much anger and fear and pain seething around the little clearing among the pine trees. It would only be worse after Teasel led them in sending Sorrel's body out on to the river in their mourning ritual. Then the otters would start to move from grief to revenge.

'Why didn't Lady River just tell *everyone* we had to stop fighting?' Silken asked, shivering, as they watched Teasel argue with the others. The grizzled otter was stamping a paw against the sandy ground, kicking up dust and pine needles. The fur stood on end all around her neck and shoulders. She was furious, they could all see it. They had no chance of persuading *her* to walk away from a battle. 'I don't see why she only told us.'

'I don't think everyone can hear Lady River speaking to them,' Sedge said thoughtfully. 'Teasel told me that once. That only those beloved of the river even get to catch a glimpse of her. Perhaps Teasel and the others just can't bring themselves to listen now. Perhaps she spoke to us because we were the only ones who would hear.'

'The sun's going down,' Teasel called. 'It's time.'

Sorrel's body lay at the edge of the water, on a raft lightly woven from willow twigs and strewn with flowers. He was curled up as if sleeping, his eyes closed, and he looked entirely peaceful.

The otters gathered in a half-circle around the raft, and the beavers came to stand among them, a little hesitantly, as if they weren't sure they were welcome. But there were nods and outstretched paws, and soon the whole line was linked together.

'Lady River, we ask you to care for our brother,' Teasel said slowly. Her voice shook a little, but it grew stronger as she carried on. 'Take this empty shell, and leave us with our memories of Sorrel.'

'Sorrel . . .' whispered all the otters, and the whisper hushed out over the water as Teasel gently pushed the raft into the current. It should have moved swiftly away downstream, but instead the little raft held still in the middle of the river. For a moment, Sedge thought that it had caught on a rock –

but then he saw the gentle swirl of the water around the raft. The line of otters and beavers whispered and pointed as a silver-white head and paws appeared out of the water, and pulled Sorrel's body smoothly under. The empty raft bobbed away down the river, and a few petals spun lazily on the surface.

'He's gone,' Teasel whispered. She sounded surprised, almost shocked, as if she hadn't believed it until then. Sedge tightened his grip on the old otter's paw and Teasel looked at him gratefully for a moment. Then she shook herself and straightened up, glaring round at the otters and beavers gathered at the edge of the water. 'And now we do our utmost to avenge him.'

Teasel spoke for all the otters, it seemed. No one wanted to listen when Sedge and Silken and the younger beavers tried to plead for peace.

'Lady River spoke to us!' Silken protested, glaring at Teasel. 'It was an order!'

Teasel sniffed. 'Just because you two have seen Lady River once, it doesn't mean you can claim her authority for every little whim. You're not leading the holt yet – either of you.'

Silken sucked in a furious breath, ready to tell Teasel exactly how wrong she was, when Sedge broke in hurriedly.

'It's true, Teasel. We all saw her, Frost and Speckle and Brindle too. She was *angry*. Fighting among the creatures of the river, it's wrong – she told us so.'

'We are not fighting creatures of the river, though, are we?' Their father stared down at him, creases of disappointment marking his muzzle. 'We are fighting foxes. Strangers. Violent, *angry* strangers who have marched on to holt lands – and killed your own mentor, Sedge. Tonight is for us all to honour Sorrel and mourn his loss. But then we must fight! How can you argue for peace now?' He shook his head and an angry murmur ran around the listening otters. The beavers gathered around Sandy.

'It's not like that,' Frost rumbled, stepping up to stand beside Silken, with Brindle and Speckle standing close behind them. 'Silken and Sedge are right. She doesn't see the foxes as strangers, now that they're living by her river. We're poisoning her waters by fighting, that's what she said.'

'By fighting we're protecting the river!' Teasel roared, and Campion turned his back on his cubs.

'You young ones should leave us now,' he said to them over his shoulder. 'You don't understand what you're saying.'

Silken shared a desperate look with Sedge – and then the pair of them sloped away to the water's edge, with Frost, Speckle and Brindle hurrying after them. They huddled miserably on the bank, looking out at the river.

'If only she'd tell us what to do,' Silken whispered.

'I – I suppose she doesn't want to have to. We're supposed to work it out for ourselves. But I don't see what we *can* do, now.' Sedge worried his paws together, and for once Silken didn't tell him to stop. 'Why won't they listen?' he added, his voice deepening to an angry growl. 'How are we ever supposed to lead the holt, if we can't make them understand?'

Silken was silent. 'I suppose if we can't make them understand, we shouldn't be the leaders,' she said at last. 'Not that I want to be anyway,' she added, glancing at Sedge. *But – I don't want to live at the holt and have someone else telling me what to do when I don't agree with them either*, she thought, gazing at the dark water. *I suppose it would be all right if it was Sedge . . . What if everyone feels like that, though? How will we ever know what the right answers are?* She shook herself. Now wasn't the time to worry about that.

The five of them slept close to the water that night, a little away from the main gathering around the fire. It was odd to feel unwanted and apart, just as she had at the Stronghold, but at the same time to be curled up and sleeping in a warm mass of fur with her brother and three beavers. They were apart, together.

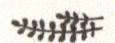

The next day, Sedge and Silken took Brindle with them when they were sent off scouting for back ways into the foxes' camp. Sandy had ordered Frost and Speckle to go foraging, but she seemed to have forgotten about the smallest beaver kit. Or she had ignored him on purpose.

'She wants to keep you away from each other,' Sedge murmured to Silken, as Frost cast a regretful look back at them.

'I'm not surprised, after yesterday,' Silken replied darkly. 'She thinks we're leading them astray.' She nudged Brindle, smirking a little. 'You're astray already.'

Sedge glanced round at the small beaver, wondering how he'd take the teasing, but Brindle snorted, and shoved her back, almost affectionately.

'You're better off with us,' Sedge told him as they set off. He was watching his words, trying not to sound pitying. Brindle was prickly and snappish. He reminded Sedge of Silken when they'd first met far down the river. But still, he admired the kit. He had been brave enough to break away from Tawny, and no one seemed to be giving him much credit for it. Sedge knew how hard it was to go against family.

'I don't think we'll find anything useful along here,' Silken muttered. Teasel had sent them across the river to investigate the bands of rocks on the other bank, further upstream. She thought perhaps the foxes had a sentry post in among the rocks somewhere. 'Teasel and Campion just want us out of the way so they can carry on making plans for an attack.'

Brindle nodded as he picked his way around a boulder slippery with moss. 'Now you know what it feels like to be shut out.'

'I grew up feeling like this,' Silken snapped back. 'Remember? I was the odd one out at the Stronghold, always. At least you know what you are.'

'I suppose,' Brindle agreed reluctantly. 'Sorry.' He turned away from Silken, looking embarrassed, and plunged ahead between two rounded boulders. Then he stopped with a squeak.

'Did you slip?' Sedge called. 'You've got to be careful – *Oh.*' He stopped, staring over Brindle's shoulder at what was hiding in the damp hole between the boulders.

There wasn't a fox sentry post – but there was a fox. Her bright fur blazed against the greyish stone, and she was staring back at them in fury.

'Brindle, get away,' Silken screamed, dragging at them both, her paws slipping and skidding in her panic. 'Get back away from her, Sedge! Run! *She killed Sorrel!*'

Brindle stumbled back just as the fox reared up between the boulders, eyes glittering with malice. She launched herself at the three of them, claws outstretched and hissing – and then they realised why she'd been hidden there, curled up in the dark cleft.

She could hardly move. One of her front legs was sticking out at an odd angle and she was covered in cuts and torn fur. She collapsed back against a rock, her muzzle curled away to show her teeth – fearsomely long, and sharp as the otters' stone knives. Her hiss had deepened to a low, angry growl, but she was *frightened*, Sedge realised. There was a flash of white showing at the very edge of her eyes, and she was trembling with fear, or perhaps from the pain of her leg, he couldn't tell. Probably both.

There were three of them and one of her, and she was injured. It was the perfect opportunity to capture one of the enemy and bring her back to their camp. Where . . . where what would happen? Sedge could imagine what Teasel and Campion would want to do, still burning with their anger and misery over Sorrel's death.

'She's hurt,' Silken whispered to him, and Sedge nodded.

'I know.' He hesitated, thinking. 'We should take her back with us.'

'Yes.' Silken swallowed hard and looked back at the river, racing past the rocks in a summer glitter of tiny ripples. 'Or we could . . .'

'What?'

Silken's muzzle wrinkled with worry. 'Lady River said we

were supposed to end the fighting. And then we find *her*, here. Just waiting for us.'

'It's like a sign.' Sedge nodded. 'You asked how we were meant to stop it, and Lady River sent us a way.'

'Are we going to give her back to the foxes?' Brindle asked, his eyes wide.

Sedge looked at Silken. 'She tried to kill you and then she *did* kill Sorrel. Can we really set her free?'

Silken's whiskers were trembling, but she nodded. 'Yes. I can if you can. Sorrel was your teacher, after all. You'd known him so long, and she took him from you.'

'You two do go on,' Brindle said impatiently. 'We can't take her anywhere with her leg like that, you know.' He leaned a little closer, peering at the strange angle.

'Get away from me,' the fox snarled, her voice high but grating. 'I'll gut you. Run!'

The two otters and the beaver kit eyed her warily, and at last Brindle said, 'I don't think you could. How long have you been hiding in these rocks? Ever since the fight yesterday? Your leg is broken, I think.'

'You're not taking me anywhere,' the fox shrieked.

'Sssshhhh!' Sedge scowled at her. 'Do you want to bring the rest of them down on us?'

She blinked uncertainly. 'Who?'

'The rest of our party.' Sedge sighed. 'It's difficult to explain, but right now you're a lot safer with us.'

The fox didn't appear to think so. She thrashed wildly, trying to fight her way out from between the rocks, as if she thought she could bowl them out of her path and escape. She got almost as far as Brindle, who jumped back with a yelp, before her leg went out from under her and she crumpled to the ground, unconscious.

'Well,' Sedge said gloomily. 'At least that makes working on her leg easier.'

'*Can* you do anything for it?' Silken asked. 'I think Brindle's right – it looks broken to me.'

'Broken, or pulled out of its socket. I need to see it properly.' He looked round, spotting a patch of thin grass further up on to the bank. 'You'll have to help me carry her.'

The fox turned out to be surprisingly light, her bones thin under a lustrous coat of golden-orange fur. Sedge found it hard to touch her, though, remembering what she had done.

They laid her on the grass and he felt carefully around the damaged leg, trying to work out what was wrong. It was difficult – foxes and otters were not the same shape at all – but he was pretty sure the leg was dislocated. Probably the fox had fallen badly, or been thrown hard against something in the fight, and her leg had popped out of its socket. He couldn't imagine how she'd managed to get this far from the clearing where the fight had taken place. She must have dragged herself all the way across the river, in agony.

It was a good thing that she'd fainted, Sedge thought. A fox that determined might still try and take on the three of them, even with a useless leg.

'Can we help?' Silken asked. She looked a little ill, Sedge thought. He supposed that the fox's leg was an odd sight. He found it interesting and terrifying at the same time – it was a mystery he had to solve, but he was worried that he was only going to make things worse.

'Um, maybe,' he murmured. 'I wish I had Sorrel's bag. She needs willow bark, and comfrey, and – wait . . . Could you sing to her?'

'What?' Silken blinked.

'You know your songs are different, Silken. Tawny said that you were working a binding, back at the Stronghold, and I think she might have been right, in a way. Sing the pain away for her. Keep her sleeping, while I put her leg back to rights.'

CHAPTER TEN

Silken gazed down at the fox's narrow, pointed muzzle. Her teeth were showing, so that she seemed to snarl at them still, even in her stupor. She looked so strange and fierce. Did they have anything in common at all? The beavers had loved Silken's songs, and the birds sang them up and down the banks, but they were all water creatures – they had the river and the currents and the rain and the dark pools in common. Did she have anything to share with a fox?

The floods, she thought uncertainly. Loss of her home. Setting out for unknown places – she certainly understood that. 'I'll try,' she whispered, settling by the fox's head as Sedge continued to examine her.

Rest there in the grass now
Let my brother heal you
We may be strangers
But we mean you no harm

Rest there and sleep sweetly
Let my brother heal you
I beg Lady River
May my song work its charm

Silken sang softly into one of the fox's huge ears, thickly furred and lily-shaped – so unlike her own neat little water creature's ears. She repeated the words over and over like a lullaby, swaying slightly from side to side as she sang. She thought of a mother singing to her cubs – as surely as their own mother had sung to her and Sedge, though she couldn't remember it.

'Good, good, keep going,' Sedge murmured, nodding. 'Don't stop, Silken. I need to put the joint back in now. Sing to her.'

Silken shuddered and sang on as Sedge braced himself against Brindle, twisted the fox's leg in a strange little circle, and pushed. There was a definite click as the bone slipped back into place, and Silken closed her eyes and determinedly kept singing. The sound had made something in her middle turn over.

'Did it work?' Brindle asked hopefully.

'I think so. But I'm not sure she's going to be able to walk on it straight away. It's been out of place almost a day, and it must be bruised. Maybe torn up inside. She needs to rest it a while.' He sucked in his breath sharply. 'She's waking up! Silken, move back. She might bite.'

Silken wriggled away as the fox's eyes fluttered open. They were darker than they had been the day before, when she had leaped towards Silken and Sorrel. Pain had swollen her pupils till only a faint ring of amber showed. She gazed up at them, suspicious and angry. 'What did you do?' she hissed. 'My leg . . .'

'He mended it,' Silken told her. 'He put the bone back.'

The fox looked down at her front leg. Slowly, she flexed her delicate paw back and forth.

'Don't stand on it!' Sedge yelped. 'Not yet. It needs to settle.'

'Can you walk on three legs?' Brindle asked curiously. Silken and Sedge stared at him, and so did the fox.

'Perhaps,' she muttered. 'It hurts,' she told Sedge accusingly.

'It will,' he agreed. 'You put it out of the socket.'

The fox snorted. 'That great pale otter put it out, not me. He threw me into a tree.'

Silken decided not to tell her that the pale otter was their father. 'You can't complain that he fought back,' she pointed out. 'Your kind attacked first. A fox savaged the old swan, Vane, and he never did anything to you! And you killed our healer,' she added softly.

The fox looked down at her leg again, and then up at Sedge, suspiciously. 'So what are you?'

'A healer's apprentice, and you should be grateful,' he snapped back. He was shaking, Silken noticed. She doubted he'd ever done anything like that on his own before, and now shock was setting in.

The fox sucked in a thin, painful breath. 'You must want something from me. Like she just said –' she glared at Silken, narrow-eyed – 'I killed your healer. We're enemies. Why didn't you kill *me* when you could?'

Silken watched Sedge shrug. 'I'd rather mend things than break them,' he said. 'I've killed before, and I don't want to do it again.'

The fox raised one side of her muzzle, but more in disbelief than anger. Then she heaved a deep sigh, and wriggled herself half upright, sitting on her back legs, the injured front leg held carefully off the ground. 'I know, I know. I won't put any weight on it.' She looked around at the patch of grass, the rocks, and the river rushing past in the sunlight – and then back at the three of them. 'So. Am I your prisoner then?'

Silken and Sedge exchanged a glance, and Sedge gestured with a weary paw, telling Silken to go ahead.

'No,' Silken began slowly, 'we don't want to keep you a prisoner. We want to stop the fighting between us and the foxes. We'll help you get back to your camp. But we'll have to be sneaky about it, because—'

'Because the rest of the otters want to tear you limb from limb,' Brindle said. He sounded quite cheerful at the thought, and the fox looked worried for a moment.

'Ssshhh,' Silken told him. 'You're not helping.'

'At least he's honest. I think.' The fox peered down her long nose at them. 'If you want to stop the fighting, just go away. No one's making you fight us. You were the ones who came to *our* camp.'

'No, you're in *our* holt lands! And getting closer to our home every day!' Sedge sounded desperate, Silken could hear it in his voice, and it seemed the fox could hear it too.

'You're that frightened of us?'

Silken shifted uncomfortably. It wasn't easy to tell someone that they were a violent, murdering beast. 'Foxes – are very different from otters and beavers,' she said diplomatically.

The fox glanced at Brindle. 'I can understand that a barkeater would find us frightening,' she said slowly. 'But otters hunt. You eat fish and frogs. You're not so different from us. We hunt to eat, just like you.'

'But we don't *enjoy* it!' Sedge cried.

Silken wrinkled her muzzle. She wasn't sure that was

quite true. She hadn't enjoyed fishing while she still thought she was a beaver – when she had believed that it was strange and wrong, that she should be eating bark and plants. But now, now that she understood she was an otter, and fishing was what otters were made for, she loved it. Hurling herself through the water, spinning and turning on her tail, chasing the tricksy fish out of their hiding places among the water weeds. She eyed Sedge doubtfully. She fished with him almost every day, and she was sure he felt the same way she did. Was he lying? Or just trying to make himself sound different from a fox?

'Ha. She knows that's not true!' the fox crowed, and Sedge glared at Silken.

'All right.' He sighed. 'Maybe. But we kill for food, not sport like you and your kind!'

The fox put her head on one side. 'How many foxes have you ever spoken to?'

'Well. Only you,' Sedge admitted. 'But I've heard stories.'

Brindle snorted. 'You sound like my mother.'

The fox glanced between them curiously, and Brindle leaned forward. 'My mother really hates otters,' he explained. 'She didn't want us to be on peaceful terms, and she tried to get our whole lodge riled up about it.' Then he seemed to realise how close he was to the fox's teeth, and froze.

'Your friend just mended my leg,' the fox said. 'I'm not going to tear your throat out. Not yet, anyway.'

Brindle nodded nervously.

'What stories do otters tell about my kind?'

Silken took in a slow breath. What should she say? Surely not the truth. But maybe the truth was the only way. 'Our elder, Teasel – she's here with us, at the clearing – she had a friend stolen by foxes. They killed her, and Teasel found her body. She said that the foxes killed Blossom for the fun of it.'

'We kill for food. Just like you.'

'But—'

'I'm not claiming that no fox ever killed for the wrong reasons, mind you. But one fox isn't all of us.'

'Mmm.' Silken stopped, not sure what to say.

'You threw stones at our envoys,' Sedge pointed out.

'They came stealing into our camp! How were we to know what they wanted?' The fox sighed. 'You don't understand what has happened to us, these last two changes of the moon.' She shifted, easing her injured paw, but Silken thought it might be memories that were really hurting her. 'There was a great flood further up the river, two springs ago. You know of this?'

'The same for us downriver,' Silken said.

'Our den was safe – we lived far enough away from the

river – but we watched the waters tear away the banks. The shape of the river changed, and we thought ourselves lucky that we had a strong, solid den, well away from the bank. No water could harm us.' She stopped, sighing again. 'Then this spring, it happened again. So much water, hurling itself along the course of the river from the very heights of the mountains. This time, the river carved a new channel – or broke open an old one, perhaps.' She shuddered. 'It was so fast. We'd seen the waters rising, but we didn't understand. Our den was swept away in a night. Destroyed. And half my clan with it.'

'Oh . . .' Silken whispered, remembering the flood surge that had nearly stolen Sedge, just when she'd found him again.

'We were scattered across the forest, lost and desperate. One by one we found each other again. Those of us who were left,' the fox added bitterly. 'That whole patch of the forest is strange and different now. The earth shakes and hills slide. We couldn't stay. So we set off to find a new den. Is it any wonder that we're frightened, and angry, and we lashed out when you came creeping into our piece of wood?'

The two young otters stared at her, remembering the moment when they'd rounded the bend of the river and first seen Greenriver Holt abandoned in the floodwater. Their home had gone – or so they'd thought. Silken's memories of the holt had only just started to return, and then it had been snatched away from her. They hadn't known what had happened, how many otters had survived. In the end only one otter had been overcome by the flood, an elderly gatherer named Yarrow, and the holt was salvageable, with work. Even the stores had been mostly saved. They had been so lucky. But that moment of terror and loss was still inside her – she woke up in the night sometimes to find it happening all over again in her head.

And it had really happened for the fox.

'We'll take you back to your camp,' she said again, slowly. 'I'm just not sure how we do it.'

'A raft?' Sedge suggested.

'A what?' the fox eyed him suspiciously. 'What are you talking about?'

'We can't carry you,' Sedge explained. 'But we could put you on a raft and swim you along the river.'

'Swim!' The fox darted a horrified look at the water.

'Don't foxes swim?' Brindle asked. 'How did you get this side of the river?'

'I was running away from the fighting,' the fox admitted. 'My leg – I didn't understand what had happened to it, and I was frightened, and all I could think was to get away. There seemed nowhere else to go, so I went into the water. The river isn't deep, just here. Most of the time the water only came up to my chest.' She shuddered. 'I still didn't like it. I could feel it wanting to carry me away. Although it did ease the pain of my leg.'

'The water would have taken some of your weight,' Sedge agreed. 'It would have been easier than walking on land. You wouldn't have to get in the water this time, though. We'll build a raft out of sticks – that's all a raft is, sticks tied together. You lie on it, and we'll pull you upriver to the fox camp.'

The fox licked at her muzzle. 'You shouldn't,' she murmured reluctantly. 'You might not want to capture me, but the rest of my clan won't be so generous to you. You'll be putting yourselves in danger, going anywhere close.'

Sedge looked at Silken and Brindle. 'We'll do it anyway. We have to.'

The fox gave her head a slow shake. 'I don't understand you. Not at all. Why would you do that?'

'The river told us to,' Silken explained. 'We see her. Not very often. But we're creatures of the river, and she talks to us. She told us that fighting poisons her waters, and she said we had to stop it, after Sorrel died. Sorrel was our healer,' she added quietly. She didn't say, *The one you killed*. She didn't have to. The words were in the air between them all.

The fox shifted her weight again, looking uncomfortable, but curious. Thoughtful. 'We don't have a river to talk to us. But there is a fox we see in the fire flames, sometimes. She was the one who gave the clan the message to move on and find a new place for our den. If your river spirit is like that, then I see why you want to help me.' She shivered. 'I'll lie on this raft.'

'It won't take long,' Silken promised her. 'Longer to build the raft than to carry you back.'

Silken was right. It was all very well to say that they would build a raft, but none of them had ever tried to make one, and it was fiddly. Brindle went foraging for the wood, while Sedge and Silken braided stringy rush fibres to tie the pieces together. The fox watched them all, somehow managing to look superior about the whole thing despite the fact she was the one being rescued.

'It only needs to last round a few bends of the river,' Silken muttered, looking at the birch branches that Brindle kept trundling back with, but the beaver kit was clearly enjoying himself, measuring the branches by eye and trimming the ends so that they lined up perfectly. He kept fussing about the design, demanding that Sedge and Silken tie branches across the raft to brace it, and complaining that the rush twine wasn't strong enough.

The finished raft was rickety, and fragile-looking, and the knots were loose, but it held together when the two otters swam it out into the river, and the fox hopped after them, grumbling rebelliously to herself – though Silken was sure that was to cover up her fear.

'Wait!' Silken called, as the fox hesitated at the water's edge. 'Before we do this – we don't even know your name.'

The fox tilted her head. 'I am Ember,' she said, her voice only just loud enough to be heard over the water beating on the stones.

Sedge bit down on the twisted rushes again, trying to ease the drag on his mouth. How had the raft otters managed this all the way up the river from Oak Island, and with their raft so heavily laden? His teeth felt as if they might fall out.

'Not much further,' Ember told them eagerly, shifting on the raft as if she were trying to stand up. It rocked beneath her, and Brindle lifted his head out of the water and growled, 'Don't wriggle!' He was pushing the raft from behind, and from the sound of it, that was just as uncomfortable as pulling.

'Someone's seen us, I think,' Silken hissed, tipping her head sideways. They caught a glimpse of a white-tipped tail vanishing among the pine trees. A fox scout, on the way to announce their arrival.

By the time they drew up where Ember directed them,

against a flat rock that jutted out into the water, there was a ring of foxes waiting, staring. Sedge and Silken scrambled on to the rock, still gripping the braided rushes in their mouths, and Brindle shoved the raft hard up against the side. Ember wriggled so that she was sitting upright.

There was a faint splash, and then another and another, and Sedge saw that four heavily built foxes had jumped into the river, swimming clumsily around behind him, Silken and Brindle – cutting off their escape. He had expected something of the sort, but the river felt suddenly colder all the same, as if he'd dived into the deepest of shaded pools. He and Silken could probably outswim the foxes, who weren't built for water, but he wasn't sure about Brindle, and they weren't leaving the kit behind.

A large fox with the same bright fur as Ember flung herself between Silken and Sedge, lying flat on the rock and nuzzling joyfully against her, and then sniffing at her injured leg. She snarled at the two otters. 'What have you done to her?'

'Nothing! They brought me back!' Ember cried. 'You ought to be grateful.' She bowed her head respectfully to an even larger, dark-furred fox. 'Call off the guards, Cinder. Let them go.'

'Let them go? Have you forgotten that they attacked us?' the dark fox growled.

'Their river spirit let them find me hidden among the rocks. No foxes had searched me out.'

Her mother let out a miserable whine. 'After the battle Flame and Brand were sure that they'd seen you in the river, struggling against the pull of the water. They thought your leg was broken . . . They said you went under. We thought you were gone, we were grieving.' She lowered her head submissively towards the two otters. 'I thank you for bringing me back my cub.'

'This river spirit . . .' The dark fox narrowed his eyes at Sedge, Silken and Brindle.

Sedge dropped the rush rope from his mouth and held it against the rock with his paw instead. 'We call her Lady River. We see her as an otter, and other river creatures have seen her too.' He nodded towards Brindle. 'We think she helped us find Ember. She told us that we have to stop fighting with each other. Anyone who lives close to the river belongs to her, you see? That's how she thinks.'

'And this is why you brought our young fox back to us?' Cinder said slowly.

Sedge nodded. 'We didn't know how we could find any way to meet with you peacefully, until we found Ember. To us, she seemed like a message from Lady River.'

There was a confused, uncomfortable whispering among

the foxes, and the fur prickled along Sedge's spine. Would they ever understand? He took a deep breath, wondering what to call the fox who was clearly the leader of this clan. Just Cinder seemed too familiar. 'Lord Cinder,' he began, padding his paws against the rock uncomfortably as the foxes snickered. Perhaps that was wrong. He didn't care. 'Ember told us about your den. Your great loss.'

The whispering changed to a low growl, and Ember laid back her ears.

'Did she indeed,' Cinder said flatly.

'Our holt was flooded too,' Sedge murmured, staring down at his paws. 'We were cast out, and one of our otters was taken from us. Still, we were able to return. There have been otters at Greenriver for so long, we couldn't imagine how it would be to lose our holt. My mother was ready to lead us away if the water rose any further, but it would have broken her, I think.' He looked up at Cinder and the other foxes, seeing their lowered heads and flattened ears, the glimpses of teeth. 'I'm sorry,' he said.

'You want us to believe in a river who's demanding peace,' Cinder answered him. 'When it was your river who destroyed our den and stole half our clan.'

Sedge gulped. 'Something went wrong. The river changed – or we did. No one knows. We lost the love between the river and the otters, but now we have it back. She has promised no more floods.'

'It's too late for us,' Cinder growled. 'Our den is already lost. Our families are gone.'

Silken stepped a little closer, moving her rope under her paw so she could speak. 'But how will fighting us help? That can't be the answer. More of us will die, and more of you! How can that be right when you've lost so many already? Why should foxes have to be against everyone else? These are our lands – they have been for as long as otters can remember.' She swallowed. 'But if you settled here peacefully, or – or even closer to our holt, it wouldn't actually make any difference to us. Not unless you choose to keep on fighting.'

Sedge shifted uncomfortably, but Silken was right. Foxes didn't eat the same things as otters. It was just the feel of it. The idea of them close by, after all those stories from Teasel, all the whispers. Silken was happier to trust than he was, perhaps from her experience growing up among other creatures. But Sedge kept remembering the life pumping out of Sorrel under his paws.

They were angry, he told himself. *They were grieving. They thought we were a threat.* And then, miserably, *They didn't know Sorrel. If we hadn't been strangers. If otters hadn't kept themselves apart for so long . . .*

'No,' said Cinder at last. 'We're grateful that you brought Ember back to us. We'll let you small ones go back to your own. But tomorrow,' he went on sternly, 'tomorrow we must carry on travelling down the river, searching for a place to make our own. And we will fight anyone – otter, beaver, *anyone* – who stands in our way.'

Ember stood up on the fragile raft, then hopped on to the rock between Sedge and Silken. 'They risked their lives to rescue me and bring me back to you. Doesn't that tell you anything about the kind of creatures they are? We can trust them. And I saw their river spirit.' She nodded wildly as Sedge and Silken swung round to stare at her. 'I did! While he mended my leg, his sister sang to me, to keep me sleeping so the healing wouldn't hurt. And another otter came, a white otter. She looked down at me, and then her whiskers tangled with mine . . . She breathed on me.' Ember made a little growling snort and glanced shyly at the otters. 'I'd never have been brave enough to climb on to that raft otherwise.' She hobbled further forward, so that she was almost nose to nose with Cinder. 'Wherever we go will belong to someone else now. Our home is gone. Are we going to fight for ever?'

'And what should we do instead?' Cinder snarled at her.

'Ask.' Ember shrugged. 'Explain. Tell our story. Ask for help. For friendship. Or take it when it's offered.' She looked round and nodded respectfully at Sedge and Silken and Brindle – and after a moment the three of them nodded back.

'As far as I understand it, we've been offered friendship by three young tearaways who are trying to engineer a truce all by themselves,' Cinder muttered. 'And by a ghost otter you saw in a dream.' But he didn't sound as angry any more. Mostly he just sounded tired.

'I will stand by my cubs' offer,' came a low, clear voice from the water.

The foxes' heads shot up, and the four foxes in the water spun round in a mess of panicked splashing. Out in the river were Campion, Teasel and Sandy, with the rest of the otters and beavers gathered behind them.

Cinder gave the foxes in the water a hard look and stepped forward to the edge of the rock. 'You are generous. Especially as you've just proved your advantage in a territory bound by a river.'

'We came underwater,' Campion explained, with a polite nod to acknowledge the compliment. 'This is our element, you see.'

'The lady of the holt wishes us to show generosity,' Teasel said, although she did sound a little as though she was spitting the words out between her teeth. 'Our good fortune after the floods should be shared with others. She is bringing her heirs up to show that same generosity.' She glared at Sedge and Silken. 'Though it would be preferable if they had *asked* first.'

'We are – grateful,' Cinder said slowly. 'This is unexpected.'

He did look shocked, Sedge thought, and so did Ember – as though she hadn't thought her outburst would make this much difference.

'We heard our young ones speak,' Teasel told him. She still sounded gruff and reluctant, but somehow that made her more believable. She wasn't just spilling out sweet words, Sedge realised. 'They're young still, but they are growing beyond us. Things will be different when they're the elders of the holt. We should not let old memories shape our ways for ever. We must think of our young ones now, and listen . . .'

'Do you think Lady River spoke to them as well?' Silken whispered in Sedge's ear. 'I never thought I'd hear Teasel say something like that.'

'Maybe,' Sedge muttered back, but he was still staring at the foxes. At their whispering, their hopeful glances. Perhaps there really was a chance of peace.

Ember hopped a little closer to Teasel and lowered her head. 'I – I was the one who attacked your cub and killed the healer. I am sorry for it. It was in a battle, and I am not ashamed – but I am sad.'

'Healers are the best of us,' Cinder said quietly, and he moved up closer to touch Ember's muzzle with his own.

Teasel sucked in a breath and nodded. Then she said at last, 'Come and share a meal with us. At sundown. We'll fish for you – foxes can eat fish, yes?' She glanced at Ember, who nodded eagerly. 'We'll talk.'

The fur around Cinder's neck was all on end now, giving him a great ash-grey ruff that made him seem far larger than the other foxes. But he bowed his head to the old otter and said, 'At sundown then.'

'Sedge. Silken.' Campion called to them sharply, and the two young otters slipped into the water with Brindle. Sedge glanced up anxiously at their father as they drew close to him. He'd seemed so angry the night before, when they'd tried to tell him about Lady River's commands. He still looked strained around the eyes, his jaw tense with worry.

He nudged noses with Sedge, and then with Silken. 'You did well,' he murmured. 'You saw what needed to be done when we couldn't. I should never have assumed that you were just frightened cubs. I suppose it's hard for me to understand that you're as full-grown as you are, when I've hardly seen you. My own fault. That was a brave thing you did today.'

'Foolhardy,' Teasel growled, but Sedge thought that she

was proud too, though she'd probably never admit it. 'Let's hope it works.'

The time passed slowly until sundown, with fishing and foraging and worried chatter, and then they heard the slow beat of wings. Silken and Sedge sprang up, staring eagerly along the open path the river cut through the trees. Vane was gliding gracefully down to splash across the surface, and behind him was a dark mass of heads cutting through the water, otters and beavers swimming together.

'Ma!' Sedge yelped, plunging in to greet her, with Silken close behind.

Lady Thorn sniffed and nuzzled at them eagerly, anxiously. 'Has there been fighting? Are you well?' She glanced up to the bank, searching for Teasel, and Sedge saw her let out a little loving sigh as she found the grizzled otter.

'There was, Ma,' he said, feeling the words catch in his throat. He had not needed to tell anyone that Sorrel was gone, until now. 'Sorrel was – injured. I couldn't save him . . .'

Thorn's eyes darkened. 'They killed Sorrel?' she hissed, darting out on to the bank and shaking her fur into spikes. 'He was the gentlest, the kindest . . .'

'Sedge tried so hard to save him,' Silken told her.

Sedge swallowed. 'I didn't know how much he'd taught me. I'll do his work, Ma, I promise you.' He'd never seen his mother look so angry. He was used to her looking sad, and tired, but now she was seething. 'Ma, don't. Please. The fighting is over. The foxes have lost so much, they were broken. You'd understand, if you'd spoken to them.'

Thorn turned slowly to look at her cubs. '*You* spoke to them?' she asked slowly.

'They made the peace,' Teasel said, laying her paw on Thorn's. 'Your cubs. Careless and foolish, but inspired. This time,' she added, with a glare at Sedge and Silken. 'Breathe, dearest. The foxes are coming to dinner.'

'They aren't coming,' Sedge murmured, watching the last glowing light of sunset bleed into the river.

Silken peered at the surface of the water, trying to believe that she could still see pinkish clouds shining back from the darkness. 'They might!'

'There's time still,' Brindle agreed, and Frost nodded firmly. Even Speckle tried not to look too doubtful.

'But Teasel said sunset. Everything's ready, and they're not here.' Sedge looked back at the fire, the fish laid out beside it, neatly arranged on great green leaves, and even sprinkled with herbs and wood garlic. The beavers had piled fresh bark and more herbs up too, and now they and the otters were talking quietly, seriously, among themselves. Lady Thorn was deep in anxious consultation with Teasel and Master Grey. Sedge could see bitter glances cast his and Silken's way. He turned back to the river, wondering what they would do now.

He thought he saw a flash of pale fur, a small patch of silver-white against the dark water . . .

Then the fire rose a little higher as another piece of pine wood caught – and the flames reflected flickering in the eyes of the foxes. They came padding quietly through the trees, Cinder at their head and Ember hopping on three legs behind him, a bundle of sweet herbs in her mouth as a gift.

They sat down at the edge of the firelight, tails thumping slowly on the dusty ground. Cinder nodded to Teasel, to Campion and Lady Thorn and Master Grey – but when he spoke, it was to Sedge and Silken.

'We came.'

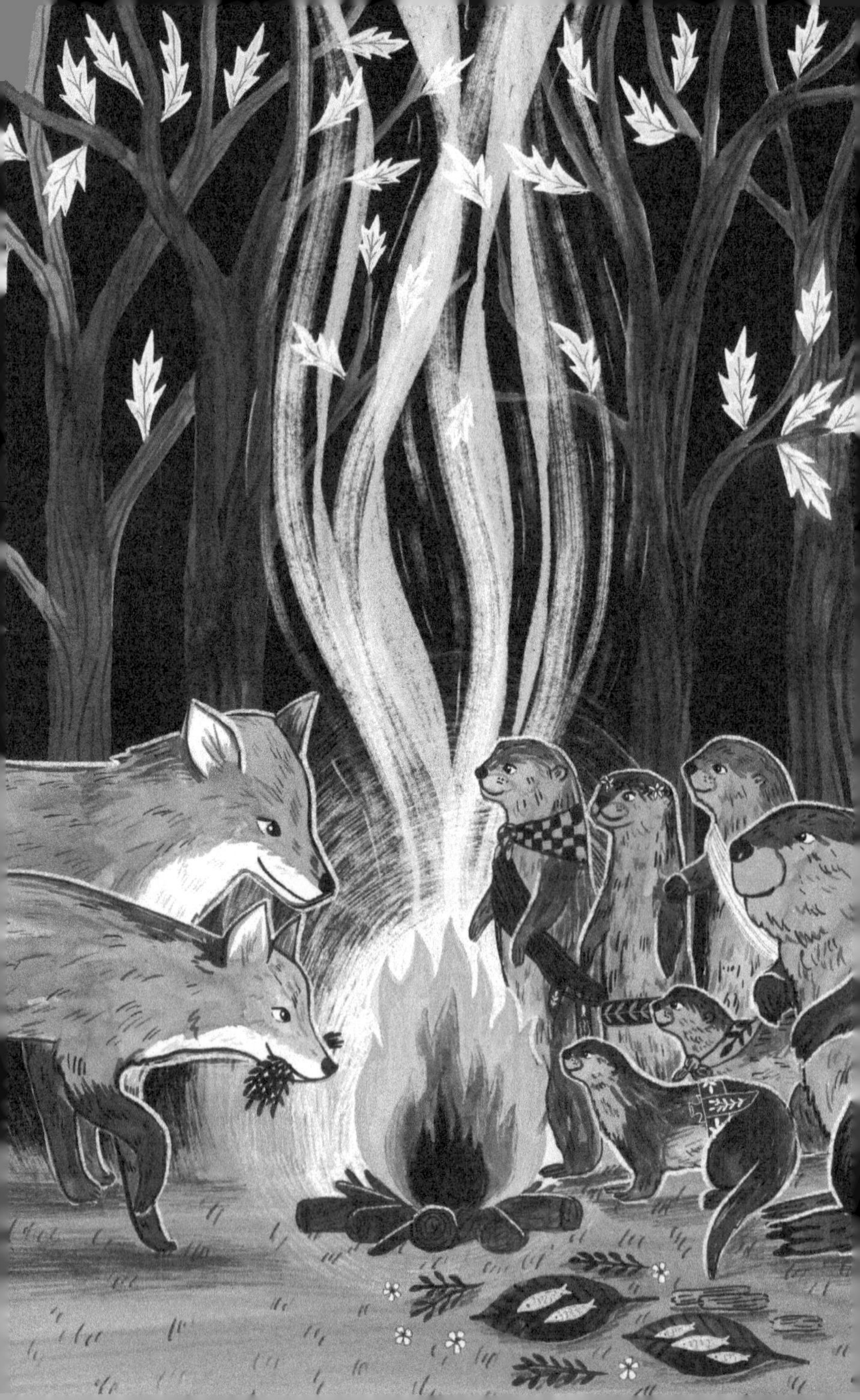

Letters, Carried Up and Down the River

To Ember, Riverbank Den

Sedge says I have to ask if your leg is properly healed. Don't forget that you won't be able to walk on it for any distance, and don't just chew willow bark and keep going because you'll only be making it worse.

He's been reading all Sorrel's old journals — there are stacks and stacks of them, piled up in the healer's chamber. He goes everywhere with his nose in a book, muttering about poultices and tinctures, and he's sounding more like Sorrel every day.

How is the new den? Do you think you'll stay close by the riverbank? I'll be sending this by a young heron who stopped by the holt to chatter on about these strange new settlers. Everyone is talking about you, up and down the river.

Send a message back by the heron — he's a gossip, he won't mind flying back here if he gets to tell us all about his daring journey to the fox den.

Silken Greenriver

To Sedge, Greenriver Holt

I'm writing to you because I still don't think your sister likes me. Don't show this to her! It's very odd being back here at the lodge without my mother and father. I've moved out of our old family chambers — they were too big and empty, they echoed. Frost let me share a room with him instead, and I suppose I quite like it, even though he snores like a bittern. Master Grey is talking about sending some of the younger beavers up the river to stay close by the holt so we can learn more about otters. I've asked if I can go, and so has Frost. Perhaps we'll be travelling upriver again in not too long.

    Brindle

What does this say?

Surely he doesn't really mean yellow water lily?

I wish Sorrel's writing wasn't so scrawly.

I keep wanting to go and ask him, and then I remember.

Ember sent a message back by the heron today — she says I should stop fussing and her leg is perfectly fine.

I suppose that means that I healed her.

decoction
yellow li[ly]
for the
of fever
must
gather
early

ACKNOWLEDGEMENTS

Thank you so much to everyone who wanted more of the story of Greenriver! I was so happy to go back into my river world. So many people have helped to bring *The Story of Greenriver* and *The Swan's Warning* into being . . .

Thank you to Lena McCauley for all your editorial suggestions – you made the story so much tighter and tenser, while also not making me panic about the edits . . .

Abie Longstaff was also generous enough to read the first draft and tell me honestly some of the many things that were wrong with it – I'm so grateful.

Thank you to Ruth Girmatsion, for desk-editing *The Story of Greenriver* and *The Swan's Warning*, and getting them both into such perfect shape.

A huge thank you to Zanna Goldhawk for the beautiful cover and illustrations – so wonderful to be able to see the river for real. Lynne Manning's design has made both books look so special.

I am terrible at titles, so I'm immensely grateful to my agent Julia Churchill for everything, as usual, but especially this time for coming up with *The Swan's Warning*!

Thank you to everyone at Orion Children's Books – and particularly to Lucy Clayton and Beth McWilliams for steering me through publicity and marketing.

Finally – thank you to Jon, Ash, Robin and Will for putting up with me muttering about otters for months again.